Cocktales & NIBBLES

—— A Collection of 12 Short Stories ——

J. S. RAYNOR

Beaten Track

www.beatentrackpublishing.com

Cocktales and Nibbles
First published 2022 by Beaten Track Publishing
Copyright © 2022 J. S. Raynor

Paperback ISBN: 978 1 78645 540 6
eBook ISBN: 978 1 78645 541 3

Cover design: Debbie McGowan

Beaten Track Publishing,
Burscough, Lancashire.
www.beatentrackpublishing.com

Contents

Foreword 1

Lite in the Sky 3

Christmas Solos 11

A Mother's Bond 27

Matter over Mind 33

A Burning Love 39

The Spider and the Fly 47

No Time for Kate 57

A Divine Love 67

Janet and John at the Hospital 75

Janet and John at the Shopping Centre 79

Help Me, Rhonda! 83

    Chapter One: Difficult Times 85

    Chapter Two: An Introduction to Rhonda 89

    Chapter Three: A Design Flaw 96

    Chapter Four: A Halloween Fright 99

A Universal Threat 103

   Chapter One: Hard Rock Hotel 105

   Chapter Two: An Unwelcome Travelling Companion ... 114

   Chapter Three: A Hard Life in Mexico 118

   Chapter Four: Teenage Tantrums 121

   Chapter Five: A Disappearing Act 129

   Chapter Six: A Chance to Escape 142

   Chapter Seven: The Awful Truth 151

   Chapter Eight: A New Way of Life 155

   Chapter Nine: A Search for Life 173

   Chapter Ten: A Long Journey 176

   Chapter Eleven: End of a Long Journey 181

   Chapter Twelve: Arrival 190

   Chapter Thirteen: Meeting Point 194

   Chapter Fourteen: A Deadly Conclusion 197

About the Author 200

Also by J. S. Raynor 201

Beaten Track Publishing 205

Foreword

I do hope that you, the most important people, my readers, enjoy these twelve short stories for adults. They range from 1,000 to 25,000 words in length. I have tried to arrange them in chronological order, starting in 1973, up to the most recent, written in 2018.

As you will discover, I do have a weird sense of humour, obvious in some of my stories.

I am, also, a hopeless romantic, which is apparent in other stories.

You may ask, why is it called *Cocktales and Nibbles*? Well, first, I can imagine you, my readers, sitting comfortably, reading these stories while, occasionally, sipping a fruity cocktail and crunching on a tasty nibble. Of course, I may be completely wrong, but imagination works wonders!

Happy reading, from John Raynor

Lite in the Sky

(January 1974)

Note from the author: This was my first story, written in 1973/74 for a short story competition. I won a certificate and the princely sum of £10.00 for my efforts.

***

The energy crisis, in the autumn of 1973, first inspired my idea. Events throughout the world had led to a shortage of natural fuels, and my country had suffered extensively as a result.

I am a naturalised citizen of the USA, although I was born in Huntingdon, England, in 1933. Being so technologically dependent, America felt the effect of such shortages more than many other countries.

I am Professor Everest, head of Technical Research in the Defense Department. Because of my responsibilities in such a role, I was fully aware of America's vulnerability to the other big powers should her energy reserves be limited.

Some proposals were simple and effective, but the majority were far too complex and unworkable. One idea was to reduce electricity consumption by introducing

'Daylight Saving Time', whereby clocks were not turned back an hour after the summer. I did not think this went far enough and set myself the onerous task of finding a more effective and worthwhile solution. If energy requirements were reduced during the daytime, then would it not be better to extend those hours rather than move them about?

Perpetual sunlight could solve many problems, and I realised, I had the means of creating such conditions. Research in my department had led to the development of high-powered lasers, primarily for military use. The intensity of these lasers far exceeded anything else in the world except for the sun.

The Japanese, who were also researching high-powered lasers, had already made an optical lens system which caused light from a laser to diverge widely yet still retain the intensity of the concentrated beam. Together, these developments could lead to a device which, if constructed as an earth-orbiting satellite powered by a nuclear reactor, would supplement the sun's energy.

Of course, it was not that simple. To create such light intensity would need a tremendous amount of research and money before it could become a practical proposition, but at least the idea now existed.

I spent all my spare time working out the details of how to make it possible before I mentioned it to an old friend of mine, a scientist engaged in highly specialised work at NASA. He was one of the few people I could trust to give me an honest and critical appraisal.

His enthusiasm was encouraging. In his opinion, there were no insurmountable technical difficulties. He suggested that I document all my findings in a report which could be submitted to Congress for approval.

Events moved very quickly after that. The Laser Intensifier and Transmitter Equipment, (LITE), as my project was called, was enthusiastically heard by Congress, and a motion was overwhelmingly supported, allocating funds for immediate use. The project had caught the imagination of all in Congress and was seen as a panacea for our energy problems, although it would take considerable time to become a reality.

I handed over all my information to the research unit, and while I was not directly involved, I kept a keen interest in their progress.

Congress had stipulated that the project should be acceptable to the rest of the world since the radiated light would affect more than just America. The proposal was put before the United Nations Assembly, which reported no objections. In fact, the project created such interest that China, Russia and the EEC suggested a combined venture covering a larger area with four Earth-orbiting satellites instead of one.

This was a big step forward in world cooperation, and although my original intention was to give America a military advantage, I could not help being pleased at the outcome.

It took three years for a research team to perfect the principle and a further seven years to construct the satellites. By the end of 1988, four huge, white monsters were on the launch pad, ready for lift-off. Each rocket was sited in a different country, and their launch times were coordinated to project the satellites into the correct orbit. I was at Mission Control in Houston and was able to watch all four rockets rise gracefully into the sky, scorching the earth with their angry, orange tails.

All launchings were perfect, and when the various stages had fallen away, the satellites were nine hundred miles above the Earth and in a stationary orbit, relative to our sun. After minor adjustments with boosters, they were in perfectly coordinated positions. Once fixed, they would automatically focus their lenses on the sun, intensify the light by laser and re-transmit it towards Earth. Power was provided by a nuclear reactor, which would only need refuelling every ten years. Each satellite would cover sixteen million square miles of the Earth's surface, providing continuous sunlight for over three-quarters of our planet.

When the lasers were energised, it was a strange yet beautiful sight as the night sky slowly became streaked with thin fingers of pale gold, reaching out, groping for the Earth. It was like lightning, viewed in slow motion. The voids slowly filled to give the sky an eerie glow as the laser built up its full intensity.

Around the globe, lavish celebrations were held. From then on, the world reaped the benefits of permanent sunlight. The oil situation had steadily worsened, because of high prices imposed by Arab nations, and a shortage of new oil strikes. In the past, humanity had plundered Earth's natural resources, believing that future generations would discover new energy sources. Now, electric lighting was only necessary when heavy cloud masses greatly reduced the intensity of light received from the satellites. So much fuel was saved that supply was, at last, able to satisfy demand.

Construction sites were able to operate on a twenty-four-hour basis without expensive floodlighting. This created a much quicker turnover in buildings and assisted the house-building programme.

A totally unexpected result of perpetual sunlight was the noticeable drop in the crime rate. The reason was, simply, that most criminal acts were previously executed under nature's mantle of darkness.

Unlike the sun, the satellites' energy had no significant heating effect, yet psychologically, it was warmer. LITE had, surprisingly, brought peace and prosperity to humankind. Even guerrilla warfare was reduced.

As instigator of the principle, I enjoyed the honours normally bestowed upon much more eminent people, with interviews for *Life* magazine and television networks.

My whole way of life was altered by this sudden exposure to the public in a way that frustrated and annoyed me. Previously, my time had been devoted entirely to science, but this mundane existence had changed to one of social gatherings and small talk. My glory, however, was to be short-lived.

I had expected some disadvantages of perpetual sunlight but considered them to be far outweighed by the benefits. I was fully aware that, after thousands of years, humans had become accustomed to sleeping during the hours of darkness and would take time to adjust. Doctors' surgeries became full of run-down, over-stressed people, their condition being emphasised by aggressiveness. Anarchists used this state of mind to propagate violence and general unrest, resulting in the deaths of thousands of people. The health of those who managed to survive the violence sank to an all-time low. Although a direct connection with perpetual sunlight was not proven, it was too much of a coincidence to ignore.

Urgent investigations were made by scientists who concluded that the metabolism would take several generations to adapt to the new conditions we had created. The inquiry also revealed that this affected more than just human beings.

Free-running animals died in large numbers and for no apparent reason. Those that did survive were of little use for food produce because of weight loss or much-reduced milk yield. This, in turn, aggravated the already serious food situation and caused the death, by starvation, of hundreds of thousands of people.

There was still worse to come. All plant life began to wither and die. Areas which had once been lush, green pastures were gradually being transformed into arid deserts dotted with the pathetic skeletons of once-proud, sturdy trees. Again, tests were carried out to establish the cause of vegetation decay. It was found that because there was no darkness, plants were being deprived of precious oxygen, so essential to life.

Poisonous carbon dioxide, exhaled by animals into the atmosphere, was formerly absorbed by plants during daylight. With plant life fast disappearing, the only prospect for all animals—humans included—was starvation and extremely agonising slow death.

Few places in the world would have escaped the terrible consequences of perpetual sunlight. The areas around the poles were not affected, but the land was not conducive to the growth of vegetable matter. In time, the mantle of carbon dioxide would spread to the whole planet and, perhaps, cause the polar ice-caps to melt, bringing even more devastation.

This tragedy is caused by forcing the laws of nature through too big a change too quickly. The world has realised its mistake too late to replace the millions of precious lives that have been lost. Lost by my inadvertent meddling with what God had intended for his children.

The satellites' have been shut down now, although they still wander through space in their endless orbit, waiting for the day when humanity is better suited to perpetual sunlight.

The rational people of the Earth are now salvaging what they can of near-extinct animal and plant life, but it is too late for many species. Never again will humans have the use of cattle to provide food or the enjoyment of eating many different vegetables. Farmers are praying that the weather will be kind for the next harvest, raised from the last remaining seeds in our possession.

Ironically, people are too occupied with struggling for survival to engage in any kind of warfare, therefore my original intention of giving America a military advantage has not been necessary after all.

There is only one person who, to everybody's mind, is public enemy number one. As instigator of perpetual sunlight, I must suffer the wrath of humankind for its devastation. I am seen as a mass murderer, overshadowing anything that such tyrants as Hitler were guilty of. I cannot blame them for wanting my life in return. They shall have their wish. The police cannot protect me forever.

I am leaving this letter of explanation as a warning to anyone else who thinks he can do better than nature.

Stuart Everest
March 13, 1995

Christmas Solos

(January 1991)

Note from the author: It was approaching Christmas 1990, and I was feeling the empty loneliness within my life following my divorce the previous year. I made an instant decision to have a Christmas break and, hopefully, find someone to share the holiday with.

***

STEVE MASON'S SECRETARY, Sue, was quite insistent. "You should go away for a holiday this Christmas. Just go away, forget about the business for a few days, and enjoy yourself for a change. You really do need a break!"

"I know I don't want to stay on my own again this year. But where could I go?" Steve had been divorced for nearly two years and frequently felt depressed by his loneliness. After twenty-two years of marriage, living on his own did not come easy.

"I'm certain I saw something in the free newspaper. Just a minute." Sue searched through the pile of newspapers and, after a short while, triumphantly exclaimed, "Found it! Yes, listen to this. 'Enjoy a luxury solos' break this Christmas. Travel in comfort by coach to Shropshire, deep in the English countryside. Stay at the four-star

Nightingale Hotel for Christmas Eve, Christmas Day and Boxing Day. Be wined, dined and entertained in absolute luxury.' There, how does that sound?"

"It may be all right. Does it say anything else about it?"

Sue read on. "It says there will be a treasure trail, fun and games and a sixties night—fancy dress and dinner dance. I wish I could go on something like that myself, but I can't afford two hundred pounds."

Steve now began to take an interest. "Two hundred pounds? It sounds quite reasonable, and if they're having a sixties fancy dress, they must be expecting people in their thirties and forties, so that would be all right." Steve was forty-four but only looked about thirty-one. He was very self-conscious about being middle-aged and had tried, as far as he could, to retain his youthful looks. "I'll phone and find out a bit more about it."

A few minutes later, Steve had booked the holiday. He had been convinced it was worthwhile when the organiser had told him that most of the places already booked were by people in the 35–45 age range and there were twice as many women as men. That ratio suited him nicely, and he hoped he could find a partner during the break. Thirty-two of the forty-five places had already been booked, so he didn't want to delay any longer and risk finding it fully booked.

Although she was a little envious, Sue couldn't help but be pleased that Steve had taken up her suggestion. "What about the fancy dress? What are you going to go as?"

"I'm not certain. Beatle or hippy, perhaps? See if you can find a place not too far away where I can hire a costume, please, Sue."

She enjoyed this type of diversion from the usual office duties and had soon found a suitable costume hire shop. A few days later, Steve was looking through many costumes, trying to find something suitable yet not too flamboyant. He eventually chose a hippy costume with bright-red trousers, waistcoat and flowery shirt. He tried the costume on and gave the assistants in the shop a laugh. *They must see some awful sights in here,* thought Steve. To complete the outfit, he bought a long, flowing, blonde wig.

He was determined to get into the Christmas spirit in an attempt to overcome his past staid and stuffy image. He did want to meet someone on the holiday who, hopefully, would end the loneliness he had endured since his divorce. If he could find a woman about ten years younger than him, this could, potentially, be a great Christmas break and well worth the expense.

When Steve arrived at the bus station pickup point on the morning of Christmas Eve, his face dropped when he realised that most of the people there were in their late fifties or sixties. He could only hope that some younger women would arrive. A good-looking woman, probably in her mid-thirties, did arrive, and Steve's hopes were immediately raised.

A coarse voice interrupted his thoughts. "I hope it's better than last year." Heads turned in eager anticipation of hearing some interesting information. The voice, which sounded as though it had been trained on fifty cigarettes a day for the last forty years, belonged to a small, elderly woman with short, grey hair. Now that she had captured the attention of all around her, she continued, "My coach was nearly involved in three accidents—if we had been a few minutes earlier, all of us would probably have been killed. There was petrol all over the road, you know!"

It was impossible to make any sensible comment in reply to such doom-ridden statements. A silent sigh must have been made by everyone present as they realised that they had been introduced to the obligatory *Job's comforter*. Steve exchanged a knowing look and a smile with the as-yet-unnamed younger woman.

By the time the coach arrived, there were still no other younger people in the group. The cases were loaded into the coach, and everyone took their seats. Steve had hoped to sit next to the only younger woman, but unluckily for him, she chose to sit next to a woman who was probably in her fifties. Steve began to wonder if this holiday was such a good idea after all, as he made the entire journey, in silence, on his own.

His hopes were raised slightly when he saw the hotel. It was modern, set deep in the heart of the English countryside and surrounded by forests and lakes. The rooms were comfortable and the staff friendly. After unpacking his clothes and changing, Steve, still apprehensive, made his way to the room where a sherry reception was to be held.

A few elderly men and women were already there, sipping sherry and speaking quietly. Steve looked anxiously around for the young woman, but there was no sign of her. He took a glass of sherry and sat next to an older woman. To his delight and great relief, the young woman entered the room and took a seat next to him.

They had only just exchanged hellos when the walking cigarette once again interrupted the conversation. "Now, everyone, I'd like to introduce myself. I'm Hettie. I think it would be a good idea if we went round the room and found out everybody's names. Then, at least, we'll all know each other a little better."

All Steve wanted to know was the name of the young woman sitting on his left. He didn't have to wait long.

Sarah, as she was called, whispered, "We seem to be the only youngish ones in this hotel."

"Yes. I was led to believe it would be mainly thirty- and forty-year-olds, but apart from us, they all appear to be in their fifties and sixties..." Steve and Sarah chatted happily for a while over their sherry and then retreated to the cocktail bar.

As they were leaving the room, they heard Hettie describing to the poor, unfortunate person who happened to be sitting next to her, in great detail, a gory operation she had recently undergone.

For Steve and Sarah, it was an instant friendship: both seemed very similar in ideas, habits and way of life, and Steve now knew he had made the right decision. Both felt obliged to be sociable with some of the older guests and struck up a conversation with a small, silver-haired woman in her late sixties called Nora. She had arrived at the hotel with a different group but, for some unexplained reason, wanted to remain separate from them. She did have a noticeable habit of repeating her conversation, in particular how many times she had travelled on the QE2, the luxury of the ocean liner and the numerous places she had visited.

When the time arrived for the evening meal, she asked if she could stay with Sarah and Steve, although, officially, the tables were organised according to the different groups.

They managed to avoid Hettie and found the other five people at their table to be quite amiable. Sarah, Steve and Nora shared a bottle of white wine over their meal and got to know each other a little better. Afterwards, they returned to the cocktail bar, and Steve asked what Sarah would like to drink.

"You know, I've always fancied but never had a Buck's Fizz. Do you think I could have one of those?"

"Of course you can! It's something I've not had myself. I'll try one as well." It could be an expensive friendship, but for a few days, Steve thought he may as well enjoy himself and, for now, hang the expense.

"Why did you come on this holiday?" enquired Sarah.

"I divorced a little under two years ago, and so last year was the first Christmas I'd spent on my own. I was thoroughly miserable and depressed and really didn't want to go through the same again this year. I must admit, though, my secretary helped me to make my decision. How about you, Sarah?"

"Very similar, really. I'm twice divorced, and my second husband walked out on me eighteen months ago. Our daughter was just two years old. It was completely out of the blue. He told me he had another woman and wanted to live with her."

"That must have been one hell of a shock," Steve sympathised. "Where is your daughter at the moment?"

Sarah's voice trembled as she replied. "Angela's with her father and his new wife. He has occasional rights of access."

Hearing the sadness in her voice, Steve realised he had touched upon a sensitive subject and made a determined effort to keep Sarah's spirits up. He enjoyed her company and felt happier than he had for a long time. At the end of the evening, they went to their separate rooms and agreed to meet up for breakfast the following morning.

***

After breakfast on Christmas Day, an adventure trail had been organised by the hotel. Sarah and Steve joined forces to answer the fairly trivial questions for the trail and, once again, enjoyed each other's company. They didn't win the trail although they answered all the questions correctly, yet neither was unduly bothered as long as they were together.

That afternoon, the weather was fine, and the duo decided to go for a walk. Near to the hotel was a large lake with a gravel path around its perimeter and through a forest. They walked, hand in hand, chatting happily for most of the afternoon, arriving back at the hotel just after dusk, their cheeks flushed from the chilling wind.

By now, the other hotel residents had become very much aware of the closeness of their relationship and exchanged knowing looks when Sarah and Steve entered the dining room together. While they conversed socially with others at the table, there was an aura of magic and happiness surrounding the by-now-inseparable couple.

There was meant to be some form of entertainment on the evening of Christmas Day, yet nobody knew what form it was likely to take. It turned out to be an amateurish copy of the television quiz show, *Mr and Mrs*.

When the compere asked for three married couples to volunteer, Steve turned to Sarah. "Shall we volunteer for a bit of a laugh? No-one's going to check if we are actually married."

Sarah giggled. "It could be good fun. Okay, I'm game if you are." They held hands as they walked up to Tony, the compere, who greeted them with a bit too much enthusiasm.

"Ah, here's a nice young couple, ladies and gentlemen. What are your names, please?" When they answered, he said, "Sarah and Steve—thanks for helping us with our little game. Tell me, how long have you been married?"

"Three weeks," Steve replied, but at the same instant, Sarah said, "Five weeks."

"That's a good start. They can't even agree on how long they've been married."

"Five weeks," Steve capitulated.

"Great! A pair of newlyweds, ladies and gentlemen. Give them a big hand, please." Tony moved on to greet and introduce the other contestants, and once they were all assembled, he asked the women to go into another room where they couldn't hear their spouse's answers. "The first question I would like to ask is, which does your wife prefer—tea or coffee?"

"Neither," Steve quickly answered. "Sarah prefers drinking chocolate." The other two men both said their wives preferred tea.

"Good. All very positive answers there. Next, perhaps something a little more difficult. I'd like you to tell me your wives' shoe size."

Steve was relieved that he wasn't the first to answer this time. He was trying to remember what Sarah had told him. When it came to his turn, he said that she wore size four shoes.

"Now, for our last question, we are going to get a bit more personal. I'd like you to tell me your wife's bra size. And I mean in inches—not hands," Tony said with a cheeky smile.

Steve was relieved at this question. He answered, "Sarah doesn't wear a bra at all." She had offered this information only a few hours earlier, and his reply created amusement among the audience.

When the women returned, only Steve had answered all questions correctly. Not surprisingly, the bra size had been the cause of difficulty for the other two men. It was then time for the men to disappear while the women took their turns to answer the questions.

"Now, ladies. If the sitting room needed decorating, who would choose the design of the wallpaper? You or your husband?"

Sarah was stuck on this one, although she knew Steve was colour-blind and so guessed she would do the choosing. She hoped he would agree with her answer.

For the second question, they had to say whether their husbands preferred to lie on the beach when on holiday or see the sights. From what Steve had said, he much preferred to see the sights.

"The last question, ladies, is what colour are your husband's pyjamas? That is, the ones he was wearing last night."

There was an air of humorous anticipation when it came to Sarah's turn, and she did not disappoint, saying with a broad smile, "He doesn't wear any pyjamas at all. Neither do I."

When the men came back, Steve's answers agreed with Sarah's. In fact, all the women answered their questions correctly, but Sarah and Steve were the only couple to answer all six questions without any mistakes. Seeing them win the contest when they had met only a couple of days ago created great amusement and a few meaningful looks among those who knew.

*****

When they met for breakfast the following morning, Steve noticed a change of mood in Sarah. She wasn't her usual cheerful self, and he wondered if he had upset her in any way. "Are you not feeling very well?" he asked anxiously.

"I'm sorry, Steve. I...I..." She burst into tears and buried her head in his chest, unable to speak.

"What's wrong? Tell me what's upsetting you?" Steve's eyes filled as the woman, whom he had only known for such a short time, held her sobbing body close to his.

"I'm sorry," she repeated. "It's Angela. I can't stand being without her. The thought of her being with her dad and his new wife is just too much for me to bear." Once again, she sobbed uncontrollably.

"I understand, Sarah. It must be awful for you." He paused, trying desperately to think of some way he could ease her agony. "Look, it's fine outside. Let's go for a long walk."

She looked torn. "I…I can't. I'm sorry, but when I feel like this, I'm not good company. I think I'll stay on my own and read the book I brought with me."

"Are you certain?" Steve asked in obvious disappointment.

She nodded in reply, kissed him and gave his hand a gentle squeeze of encouragement as she turned away to return to her room.

Steve felt sorry both for her and himself. He didn't know what to do but decided to take the long walk he had suggested, although it wouldn't be the same without Sarah by his side. It wasn't raining, but it was a very bleak, wintry day as would be expected on Boxing Day. He was wrapped up against the cold and didn't meet anyone else on his solitary walk. The strong wind whipped up the waves on the lake and the trees bent under its relentless pressure.

Steve barely noticed anything around him; he could have been walking on the moon for all the difference it would have made. How could a woman he had only just met affect him so much?

When he returned to the hotel, he spent the rest of the morning in his room, listening to the radio and feeling very low and alone. After lunch, he went into the cocktail bar and ordered a whisky and Canada dry ginger. He sat near some of the people he had become friendly with over the past few days.

"Is your wife not joining us, Steve?" one elderly man asked.

"My wife?" he asked incredulously.

"You're newlyweds, aren't you?"

Steve remembered their masquerade from the previous evening's quiz and felt heartened by this misunderstanding but avoided answering. "She's not feeling very well this morning, so she's resting in her...our room."

"Oh, I'm sorry to hear that. I hope she'll be all right for the fancy dress party tonight. You make a lovely couple—it's obvious you're very much in love."

"Thanks for the compliment." Steve smiled at this ego-boosting comment. "I'm sure she'll be better for the party." Steve's spirits had been raised, but he was still apprehensive about the evening.

"What are you coming as tonight?" the man asked.

"Ah, that's top secret—not even Sarah knows that," Steve answered with a wink. "Let's just say that I'm entering into the spirit of the occasion."

***

The fancy dress was due to start at seven-thirty, and just after seven, he telephoned Sarah's room. "How are you feeling?"

"A little better, thanks. I'm getting ready for the party. Are you ready?"

"Nearly. Would you call here on your way and give me a hand with my costume, please?"

"Yes, of course! I'm intrigued to know just what your costume is." She sounded in much better spirits, for which Steve was glad.

When he opened the door to Sarah, she fell about laughing at his bright-red hippy outfit and long, blonde wig. "That's great!" she said, giggling. "What would you like me to do?"

"See if you can improve this wig. I don't know if it will help to brush it a bit—it does seem rather tangled." Steve handed Sarah a brush, but every time she tried to brush the nylon wig, it started sliding off his head, and they both collapsed into uncontrollable fits of laughter. Eventually, they abandoned the exercise, and Sarah resorted to tying the headband in place.

As they were leaving the room, Steve realised there were no pockets in his costume to store the credit-card-sized electronic key.

"I'll keep it in my handbag if you like," Sarah offered.

"Thanks. You're looking great, by the way—I love your dress." She was wearing a very short, bright-green mini-dress, fishnet tights, big earrings and a headband.

They held hands as they walked to the hotel restaurant and were the source of great delight amongst the hotel staff and residents. Steve had difficulty keeping his wig out of the soup at dinnertime and was offered all sorts of advice and suggestions from the others at the table on how to control his lustrous golden locks. A few people, including a waitress, mistook him for a woman.

After the meal, a group played sixties style music, and the small dance floor filled with people trying to revive the jive, twist and other dances of the era. Sarah wasn't up to dancing and just wanted to listen to the music and talk. Although he was a little disappointed, Steve was grateful that he, at least, had her company.

When it came to the time for judging the fancy dress, he had great difficulty in persuading Sarah to enter the competition. Parading in front of the audience, he couldn't believe he was actually taking part. If his ex-wife could see him, she'd say he'd lost his marbles and probably disown him. The truth was, she'd been quite a domineering character who had made him retreat into his own private shell more and more over the years of marriage. Having finally emerged from that shell, he felt alive again.

It didn't help him to win the contest, however. Judging was done by comparing the applause of the audience, and since Sarah and Steve were part of just a small circle of friends, they weren't loud enough to help either of them.

Steve was still in high spirits, though, and kept the wig on for the rest of the evening, even though it was hot and uncomfortable.

Realising this was their last night at the hotel, Steve took Sarah's hand and leaned close. "I've really enjoyed this holiday, but without you, it wouldn't have been anywhere near as good." Plucking up courage, he asked, "Can I see you again?"

Sarah looked quite troubled. "I...I don't know. I'm uncertain about anything after the divorce. I've been hurt too much to make new relationships easily. Please give me time to think about it—I'm sorry, Steve."

"I understand. All I know is that I've enjoyed myself too much to go back tomorrow and not see you again. I will never forget you, whatever happens." He gave her hand a gentle squeeze, which conveyed his feelings better than any words could manage. Her eyes filled with tears as she understood the depth of his feelings for her.

One of the other people at the table interrupted their conversation by asking Sarah to pick up something they had dropped.

"Ah, you can't catch me out as easily as that." Sarah smiled. "I've had plenty of practice at picking things off the floor without exposing myself." She bent at the knees, and although the close-fitting dress stretched itself over her shapely thighs, she retained her modesty.

Just after midnight, as the party was winding down, Sarah said, "I think I'll go to bed, now. I'm feeling a bit tired. Thanks for a wonderful evening, Steve." She opened her handbag and handed him his room card-key. He thanked her for it and wished her goodnight.

Plagued by the awful feeling he would never see her again after their journey home the following day, Steve stayed and had one more drink, then excused himself.

As he walked to his room, he was thoroughly depressed. Why did such a beautiful relationship have to end so soon? He was certain she had enjoyed their time together too, but he didn't want this to just be a brief holiday romance. As he reached his room, he inserted his card-key into the lock and waited for the electronic *click* before pressing the handle. When it didn't come, he cursed himself for putting the key in the wrong way. He tried again, with the same result.

He was still muttering about how these electronic locks were not as reliable as the old-fashioned type when, slowly, the door opened. Standing there, silhouetted against the dimmed lights of his room, was Sarah.

She smiled as she took the key from him and said, "I do believe that's mine. But I think we can manage without it for tonight." Putting her arms around him, she pulled him close to her and gently closed the door.

A Mother's Bond

(January 1991)

Note from the author: After writing 'Christmas Solos', I thought about Sarah's story and wrote the following from her perspective.

***

THE MOMENT I had been dreading for the last two months finally arrived. Mike, my ex-husband, turned up at ten-thirty. We had been divorced for three years, and I still felt very bitter about the way he had just walked out on me. I'd never realised there was anything wrong with our marriage. I suppose his mistress attracted him because she was so much younger and better-looking than me. She hadn't yet experienced the dulling effect of domesticity and bringing up a family. She would soon tire of him once the initial passion had been replaced by familiarity and insensitivity. Might he do the same again if she became pregnant?

Anyway, there he was, standing at the door. He was smartly dressed, and his new wife, Shirley, was sitting in their Vauxhall Carlton, waiting for him to return with the only thing I cared for. I still couldn't understand why the courts had allowed him occasional rights of access to our only daughter, Angela. How could a six-year-old child understand why her daddy lived with another woman and was able to take her away from me when he chose to? Typical of men—what do they know about that special bond between mother and child? A few minutes of pleasure between the sheets and their job is done. Mike was certainly not a 'new man' and had never been there when I needed his support.

He smiled, gloating because he was taking away my little treasure. His smile revealed teeth which were yellowing and in obvious need of attention. I also noticed, with a certain degree of satisfaction, that there were many more grey hairs visible, both on the top and sides of his head.

"Is my little girl ready?" he asked, knowing damn well she would be. I'm sure he emphasised 'my' just to make me feel the anguish more.

I gave Angela a last hug and kiss and told her to have fun. How I managed to stop myself bursting into tears, I'll never know, but I had to retain my composure to avoid upsetting her.

It was only after I'd waved her goodbye and seen the car disappear into the distance that I could release my true feelings. I've never cried as much in my life as I did over the next few days. My eyes stung from the relentless pouring of tears—I must have looked terrible with my bloodshot eyes.

Some friends had invited me to go out to the pub with them, but I couldn't. I would've been awful company, and I didn't want to spoil their evening. No, I just wanted to be on my own and bury myself in housework.

The house seemed so quiet and peaceful, but it was an unwelcome change. Never again would I complain about the noise a six-year-old made. What I would have given right then to hear her bright, inquisitive voice.

The long, empty evenings were the worst times to endure. I would imagine I heard her crying and rush to her bedroom ready to calm her after a bad dream. Of course, it was only my imagination playing tricks on me.

Then I would stare at the empty bed, and the floodgates would open yet again, the tears streaming down my face and dripping onto my nightdress. I would pick up her favourite teddy, which she had left with me for company, she said, and I'd lie in my bed, clutching it close to me as though it were Angela herself.

When I was ironing, I would tell myself that Mike's wife could not iron as well as me. I took special pride in my ironing, and his shirts had always been crisp and immaculate when I had been responsible for his laundry. The more I thought about it, the more convinced I was that his shirts were creased, the collars not as sharp as I could make them.

What had he seen in this other woman? What did she have that I did not? I partly blamed myself for only managing to keep him for seven years.

I kept wondering if I still loved him, but no. How could I think of loving the man who had abandoned Angela and me the way he had? When Mike had been involved in a car accident two years ago, I had actually wished he would die. Death would have been a just reward for everything he had done to the two of us. I never thought

I could wish that on anyone, but I really did for Mike, who never was what could be called a careful driver.

God! Suppose he has an accident while Angela's with him! Oh, please, God, please don't let any harm come to my precious little girl!

I slept very badly for those few days, which seemed to last an eternity. The vision of Angela walking towards Mike's car holding his hand and turning to face me to wave goodbye constantly haunted me. I remember seeing her lip quiver as she, too, felt the anguish of separation.

As the time drew nearer for her return, I did not improve as one might expect. I began to wonder if she was having such a good time that she would not want to come back to me. With his money, he could afford to buy her things I could never afford on my measly income.

She would be getting lots of attention and going to all sorts of interesting places. How could I ever compete with that? *I'm sorry, Angela, for ever shouting at you when you would not go to bed. I really do love you, baby.*

At last, after six of the most miserable days of my life, the time had come for her return. Four o'clock, he'd said. Why did the time pass so slowly? *They're late. What time is it? Ten past four—where can they be? Please, please don't have an accident. Is that them now? No, it's going past.* I cursed every car which drove past my house that day.

After what seemed like hours, yet, in fact, was only twenty minutes late, Mike's car pulled up outside.

I was shaking with apprehension as I opened my door and waited for Angela to come down the drive.

"Mummy, Mummy!" she shouted excitedly as she ran towards me. She flung her arms around me. "I love you,

Mummy. Please don't let them take me again!" she cried as she hung onto me.

"No, darling. I won't. You're back with me now."

I looked at Mike. He seemed relieved to have Angela back in my care. "You win. We've had an awful time with her. She's made Shirley's life hell for the last few days. Shirley doesn't want her back again." He was almost apologetic.

I couldn't speak to him. I picked my baby up and kissed her warmly. Closing the door, I said, "Come on, darling. Let's go and say hello to Teddy."

Matter over Mind

(January 1991)

Note from the author: January 1991 was a good time for my writing, and I enjoyed putting my odd, perhaps even quirky, ideas into a form where others could, hopefully, enjoy them.

***

IT WAS PURE magic. The first time Phil Cunliffe saw the power of psychokinesis, he could not believe his eyes. He was watching Ali Shaffa, a young mystic who, although in obvious deep concentration, looked perfectly composed and relaxed.

On a table in front of the mystic, a small plastic cube slid gracefully from side to side following the movements of the mystic's hands, although there was no actual physical connection.

It was a perfectly ordinary table, and it had been checked for possible hidden magnets by a member of the audience. Another demonstration of his powers was in controlling the tilt of a plastic balance, again without any actual physical contact.

One of the most remarkable things about this so-called mystic was that Ali Shaffa was, in reality, Alan Smith, who Phil had not seen for fifteen years, back when they had been at secondary school together.

After the performance, Phil approached his old schoolfriend. "Hello, Cleavy."

Although the nickname had stuck in his mind, Phil couldn't remember why plain Alan Smith had been christened that, but at the use of his old nickname, 'Ali's' tanned face registered a mix of surprise and apprehension, followed by a faint look of recognition.

"Oh, hello… it's Cunliffe, isn't it? Yes, Cunliffe. Weren't you at Hathershaw Tech?"

"That's right," Phil confirmed. "I've not seen you for years. Who's this Ali Shaffa character?"

"A made-up name, I'm afraid. You must admit, it's a bit more impressive than plain Alan Smith."

"That's true. What's with this psychokinesis stuff, anyway? How does it work?"

Alan smiled. "I saw it on TV and thought I would try it. I never thought it would work, but, to my amazement. it actually did."

"You mean it's genuine?" Phil asked doubtfully.

"Of course it is!" Alan sounded hurt. "Providing the object is light enough and your concentration holds, it's perfectly possible to move an object by pure thought."

Phil was fascinated, but he would miss his train home if he spent any more time chatting. He asked Alan for his phone number and suggested they meet sometime for a drink.

As it was, Phil caught his train but nearly missed his station because he was so engrossed in thinking about psychokinesis and its potential. He was also trying to remember why Alan had ever been nicknamed 'Cleavy'. No doubt it would come to him in time.

Alan's stage name was much more mysterious. Glamorous even. Certainly more glamorous than Phil's career as an accounts clerk. As a thirty-two-year-old bachelor, he had a reasonable job working for a large company, but he had always been short of money. He was the sort of person who was constantly working out schemes which would make him rich and famous. The fact that he was neither rich nor famous was evidence of the failure of those schemes to date.

That night, however, Phil began to formulate a new idea that, in his mind, was bound to work. The following day, he telephoned Alan and arranged to meet for a drink that same evening.

Phil bought the drinks and then enthusiastically quizzed his old school friend about psychokinesis. He wanted to know the maximum size and weight of an object which could be moved using such powers and from what distance.

Alan couldn't give an authoritative answer to his questions and would only say there were many factors that influenced the strength of his powers. Rather than indulge in further guess work, he agreed to go to Phil's flat, which was nearby, and answer his questions using demonstrations.

Phil found several objects of different sizes, shapes and weights, put them all on the smooth surface of his kitchen table and observed while Alan tested his kinetic powers. Several of the objects proved too difficult to move.

"I wish you'd tell me what you've got in mind, Phil. You've obviously got some plan which you're not telling me."

"I'll explain shortly," Phil said and left the room to search through an old storage cupboard. After several minutes, he emerged victorious, holding a small, glass marble. Next, he carefully arranged matches on the table to form three adjacent squares and placed the marble in one of these squares.

"Do you think you could move that marble from its present square into the next one?" he asked.

"To be honest, I don't know," answered Alan. "But I'll have a try."

At first, nothing happened. Then, all of a sudden, the marble gave a little hop and jumped over the matchstick into the adjoining square.

Phil was elated. "That's fantastic!"

"I surprised myself with that one!" Alan admitted. "I didn't think I'd manage it. You'd better tell me what your idea is now."

"Have you ever been in a casino?"

"Ah." Now he understood Phil's sudden interest in psychokinesis and, although he was reluctant at first, eventually agreed to go along with his plan.

For the next few days, Alan trained as much as possible, and by the following Saturday felt confident enough to test his skills.

They agreed their plan before entering the casino. Phil was to place bets on the roulette wheel, and Alan would influence the ball to drop into the right position to achieve a win. At the end of the night, they would split their winnings and, hopefully, both walk away as rich men.

Phil had gathered most of his savings and cashed them into chips ready for the game. Alan was seated as close as possible to the roulette wheel without attracting too much attention.

Phil gingerly placed just a few chips on the red nine square.

"No more bets," said the croupier as the wheel started turning.

Phil's heart raced as he anxiously watched the wheel and the little ball spinning around its rim. He didn't dare look at Alan in case someone realised they were together.

When the croupier announced, "Red nine," Phil could not believe his ears. It had actually worked, and his winning chips were being pushed towards him.

Phil repeated this process several times, his pile of chips growing bigger as his winnings multiplied.

As was to be expected, a crowd soon began to gather around Phil as it became obvious he was on a winning streak. Each time, Phil put all his winning chips on his next bet and the people around him would cheer him on.

He was so confident of his success he hardly gave it a thought when the man who had been acting as croupier was replaced.

Phil eagerly placed all his chips on black fourteen and sat back in his seat, waiting for the winning number.

"Red twelve."

Phil's jaw dropped in disbelief. A gasp went up from the crowd surrounding him. The chips were scraped towards the banker and Phil was shell-shocked.

He turned his head to look at Alan for the first time. Alan's eyes were transfixed, but not on the roulette wheel. Phil followed his gaze and saw the cause of the distraction.

It was the replacement croupier. The casino's secret weapon was a beautiful woman with long blonde hair and a very revealing, low-cut black dress.

Phil rose and slowly walked out of the casino mourning his losses. Why hadn't he remembered why Alan's nickname was Cleavy? As a teenager, Alan had an obsessive fascination with women's breasts, particularly when they were barely restrained by a tight-fitting, low-cut dress. Clearly, this obsession had persisted into his adult life and ruined Phil's plans.

He walked away a poorer yet wiser man.

A Burning Love

(May 1991)

Note from the author: Another written in 1991—this is a tale of hope and irony, based, in part, on an unrequited love for Linda, a beautiful girl at my secondary school, when I was about thirteen or fourteen.

***

O NE OF THE most significant days in Paul Dalton's life was when he scalded his hand as a result of knocking a pan of boiling water off his cooker.

Paul was a twenty-four-year-old art student who lived on his own in a small flat and, usually, managed to look after himself reasonably well.

It was midday on Sunday when the accident happened. He was boiling an egg in his cramped kitchen when the doorbell rang. The noise made him jump, and as he turned in the confined space, he caught the handle of the saucepan, showering the scalding water over his left hand.

He never thought he could scream, but in that situation, he did so without any difficulty. He did have the presence of mind to immerse his hand in a bowl of cold water and held it there, despite the increasingly urgent ringing of the doorbell and the anxious call of a voice he recognised as his fellow student, Dave.

"Paul! What's happening, Paul?"

Wrapping a towel around his hand, Paul went to open the door.

"What's happened?" Dave asked when he saw the pain on Paul's face. As soon as Paul explained what he had done, Dave insisted on driving him to the casualty department of the local hospital.

Fortunately, the hospital wasn't very far away and had a worldwide reputation for its specialist burns unit.

As usual with all casualty departments, there was a queue of people waiting for attention. Paul assured Dave he need not wait and agreed to phone him for a lift once he'd been seen by a doctor.

It was as Paul took his place in the waiting room that he noticed her. Her shoulder-length brunette hair framed a face so beautiful and serene it took his breath away. Her slightly parted lips were full and very sensuous. She must have been the last person to enter Casualty before Paul and was sitting on his left.

Like Paul, she was obviously in pain and was clutching her left arm, around which a wide bandage had been hurriedly wrapped. She was wearing a very short skirt and sleeveless blouse, and although the circumstances of meeting were not happy, Paul was immediately attracted to her.

"Do you think we'll have long to wait?" he asked, unable to think of anything better to say.

"At least half an hour, I think." Her voice was soft and warm, making Paul's heart melt a little more.

"What's happened to you?" she asked, seeing the large handkerchief wrapped around Paul's hand.

"Oh, I tried boiling an egg without letting go of it."

Her laughter at Paul's reply caused several heads to turn in notable disapproval. Her clear blue eyes sparkled as she laughed.

"What about you?" he asked.

"A piece of charcoal flew out of the barbecue and landed on my arm."

"Ouch! I am sorry. I can appreciate how you must feel. I'm Paul Dalton." He offered his uninjured hand, and she gave it a short but welcoming shake.

"Hello, Paul. I'm Linda Scholes."

The two chatted happily until Linda was called by a doctor. In that time, Paul had discovered she was nineteen, had finished her A' levels and was having a gap year before studying English at university. They had even shown each other their burns, and much to Paul's surprise, she agreed to go out with him the following Friday to the local cinema.

It was only after she had disappeared into the examination room that Paul realised he hadn't asked for her address. He cursed himself as he was called for treatment without seeing her again.

When Dave arrived to give Paul a lift, there was little mention of Paul's injury, which was now dressed in neat bandages.

"You ought to have seen her, Dave. She was absolutely gorgeous—a good figure and a perfect smile."

"And you were so captivated by her that you did not ask her where she lived. How are you going to find her?"

"I don't know. Perhaps I should just wait outside the cinema."

Dave shook his head. "Not a good move and too risky! Can you not find her address from the phone book?"

"That's an idea. I'll have a look when I get home. She can't live far away from here."

Although Scholes was not an uncommon name, there were three numbers within the same area. Paul decided to walk near to all three addresses in the hope of spotting Linda.

The following evening, he walked to the first address but quickly discovered it was not the correct one. A couple, who looked to be in their seventies, were fussing about their tidy little garden.

Fortunately, he was in luck at the second address. Linda was just leaving the house and looked fantastic in black slacks and a white, close-fitting jumper.

"Hello, Linda. How's your arm, today?"

She looked at him blankly.

"You've not forgotten me, have you? Paul? I met you in Casualty last Sunday."

"Oh, of course!" she said. "Please excuse me. I was miles away. Er…my arm? It's a little better. Still sore."

"It will take time to heal fully. At least I understand how you must be feeling." Paul raised his bandaged hand as a sympathy gesture. "Listen, we didn't arrange where to meet when we go to the cinema on Friday. Shall I come to your house?"

"Erm…no. I'll meet you outside the cinema. What time?"

"Is seven o'clock all right?"

"Yes, that'll be fine. I'll see you then…Paul. I must dash now."

Paul made his way home again, very pleased with himself, although those few days seemed to last an eternity as he waited for his date with Linda.

When the night came, Paul took great care choosing his clothes and made certain he smelled clean and, hopefully, macho.

He was in for a surprise when he met Linda outside the cinema. She was wearing a sloppy jumper and very worn jeans. He was also surprised to notice that her hair was untidy, as it might have appeared first thing in the morning. She had far more make-up on her face than was necessary and more than Paul had expected.

"Hi, Paul." Even in those two words, he felt disappointment, as if they were said with an air of disinterest.

"Hello, Linda. How are you feeling? I mean…how's your arm?"

"Oh, that's not bad. I'm feeling bloody awful after a party I went to last night. Too much drink and acid. Have you been to any good parties recently?"

"Er…no, I haven't." Paul was stunned. As an art student, he had been through his fair share of high living, but from their chat at the hospital, he hadn't had the impression she was one for living it up. The last thing he wanted was a relationship with a raunchy, irresponsible girl who would be burnt out by the age of twenty-five.

As they walked into the cinema, he wondered if he had made a big mistake, a fear confirmed when, throughout the evening, she displayed every undesirable characteristic he could imagine.

Her language was coarse, her voice too loud, and she did everything possible to humiliate and embarrass him. She even caught his injured hand and seemed unconcerned at the extreme pain it caused him. At the end of the film, Paul knew, without doubt, it was the worst date he'd ever been on.

The biggest shock, though, was yet to come. As they were leaving the cinema, they came face-to-face with Linda's double. Paul was completely lost for words and looked first at one and then the other girl.

"You little bitch! I thought you might do something like this," said the Linda who had just appeared to the Linda he'd endured for the past two hours. To Paul, she said, "Don't mind her. She's jealous I got a date and she didn't."

"You liar! How dare you pretend to be me! Paul, it was *me* you met at the hospital, not her! She told me you met her outside the house and that you couldn't go to the cinema, tonight. Like a fool, I believed her. It was only when I saw she'd gone out that I knew she was coming to meet you."

"Don't listen to her, Paul. She'd do anything to spoil my evening."

Paul was so confused. He couldn't take it all in or work out who was who. Several people had stopped to watch the strange confrontation.

Eventually, he took command of the situation and demanded, "Right, that's enough! Stop this arguing. I want both of you to roll your left sleeve up."

The two girls meekly obeyed, but much to Paul's frustration, both of them had a bandage on their arm. After a little thought, he said, "Unfasten your bandages."

Linda's double immediately started to unravel her bandage while the girl he had been with all evening didn't even bother. As soon as he realised the implications, Paul said, "It's okay, Linda, you don't need to unfasten it any more. So, who have I been with all evening?"

Linda, with obvious relief, said, "This is Joan, my twin sister, though why she had to pretend to be me, I can't imagine. And look at those filthy clothes. You're a disgrace to the family. Just wait till Mum and Dad hear what you've done."

At that, Joan burst into tears. "Don't you know why I did it?" she sobbed. "I did it for us. I wanted to convince Paul you weren't worth bothering with."

She certainly did a good job of that, thought Paul. "But why?" he asked. "I don't understand. Why?"

"Because we're twins," Joan said. "We're meant to be there for each other for the rest of our lives. No man must interfere with that. Do you hear? No man!" With this final proclamation, Joan rushed away from them, still sobbing.

The real Linda—the soft, warm-hearted Linda whom Paul had met at the hospital, stepped up to him and put her arms around him. "I'm sorry you had to go through all that."

He held her close and kissed her gently as one of the strangest nights of his life drew to a close.

The Spider and the Fly

(May 1993)

Note from the author: In May 1993, my wife and I had been married for just one month, and what follows stems from a particularly bad experience in Manila, Philippines.

***

T HE TWO MEN in smart, blue-grey uniforms searched carefully through all the faces of the crowd of people, looking for the now-familiar characteristics. They were grateful that it was raining heavily since passengers were never as careful when they were likely to get soaked. There was no means of shelter for the many commuters emerging from Manila's busy domestic airport. As capital city of the Philippines, Manila was the hub of travel to and from the many sprawling islands which made up this fascinating, yet poverty-stricken country.

Alfredo spotted a likely client. "Look, Giuseppe— there." He pointed to a middle-aged man, who was peering through the rain. "Fourth from the left in the middle doorway."

"There's another, nearer to the right of the same doorway," Giuseppe said.

The swarthy Filipino's eyes moved to study the subject of his partner's gaze. "Ah, yes. He might be the better one to go for. He's much better dressed."

"You could be right. Come on, let's not waste time. I'll cover the man and you take care of the woman."

They strode purposefully, almost in military unison, over to the terminal's entrance, unfurling smart umbrellas as they walked. Giuseppe approached the man. This potential 'client' appeared to be in his early fifties, of medium height, with a small moustache and neatly cut greying hair, giving him a distinguished appearance.

"This way, Sir. Airport transport is just over there." Giuseppe pointed to the gleaming white taxi parked in what looked to be an official area. "Please follow me."

"Oh, right. Thank you." These few words were all that Giuseppe needed to guess the man's nationality. From his appearance, he could have been American, Australian or British, but there was no doubt that his origins lay in the latter country.

Giuseppe held the umbrella over the man's head while Alfredo protected the woman from the rain. She was much younger—by twenty years or so—than the man to whose arm she had been clinging tightly. Like many Filipino women, she was delightfully attractive, quite diminutive and with long, black hair cascading down onto slender shoulders. Her eyelashes fluttered nervously above enticing black eyes, and her lips were slightly parted to reveal perfect, dazzling white teeth, giving her a beautiful, butter-melting smile. Her free hand protectively clutched a small, black shoulder bag.

The two Filipino men took great care to provide shelter for their clients from the heavy downpour, now splashing noisily in puddles around them. As they reached the car, Alfredo and Giuseppe held the doors open for the foreigner and his young lady companion to step into the spotless, air-conditioned interior.

Once their passengers were settled, Alfredo took his place behind the steering wheel, removed a plastic card from the glove compartment and showed it to the Englishman. "This is my ID, sir. We are with airport security. You have to be very careful in Manila. There is a lot of crime here, but we will take care of you." The Englishman looked vaguely grateful. "Is it the British Embassy you wish to travel to, sir?"

"Yes, that's right, but how did you know?"

Alfredo's face broke into a broad grin, exposing many cigarette-stained teeth. His weather-beaten face made him look older than his thirty-eight years, assisted partly by several years of self-neglect. "We are used to many recently married foreigners arriving at the airport. Most of them want to go to their embassies to have their marriage papers authenticated."

"Oh, is it that obvious?" The man smiled at Alfredo's analysis of the situation.

Alfredo turned the ignition key. The engine coughed obediently into life and, as he engaged the gears, the smart-looking car slid smoothly out of the parking space, joining the streams of traffic flowing noisily along the wide roads of the Philippines' capital city.

Most of the noise was created by the drivers sounding their horns almost continuously and for no apparent reason.

Alfredo was in no hurry and eased smoothly, almost casually, through the traffic. The car was his pride and joy, taking a lot of time, effort and money to keep it in pristine condition. He hoped his clients would not notice the long detours he took to extend their journey to the embassy.

A smile of satisfaction lit his face as he looked at this newly married couple through his rear-view mirror. Over the years, he and his partner had provided transport for many such couples of differing nationalities. No matter whether they were British, American, Australian or German, they had all fallen victim to his money-making scheme.

As he studied the couple, Alfredo noted there was something vaguely familiar about the man, yet he dismissed the thought, since a lot of foreigners looked very much the same to him. It would not be long before the Englishman asked the usual question.

Almost on cue, the foreigner asked, "How much is the fare to the embassy?"

Alfredo produced a small, official-looking chart. "This is our scale of charges, sir. From the airport to the embassy is ninety dollars, or if you would prefer to book as a return journey, then it is one hundred and forty dollars." He waited excitedly for the expected response.

"Ninety dollars? You must be crazy!"

"I'm sorry, sir, but those are the official charges set by the airport authorities," Alfredo responded calmly, knowing he was fully in control of the situation. He did not care whether they were convinced by this lie. No matter how angry his client may become, the money would be paid.

"But I don't have that sort of money for a taxi!" the Englishman protested with increasing hostility. "What if I can't pay that much?"

"Oh, I'm certain that you can, sir. But if you can't, we will be quite happy to accept jewellery as payment." In a voice without any emotion, he added, "I see your wife is wearing some very beautiful earrings and an elegant necklace."

The young woman looked anxiously at her husband.

"Stop this taxi at once!" shouted the Englishman. "I am not going to be threatened by Filipino taxi drivers! You're just a pair of bloody crooks!" He made a move to open the door.

To add to the man's frustration, the car's central-locking system ensured he was effectively trapped. Similarly, the electric windows were rendered useless from a control panel in the front of the car.

"This is ridiculous! Who do you think you are?"

It was time for Giuseppe to make his move. He turned in his seat and pointed a small revolver at the young bride. "You ask who we think we are. I'll tell you. We are just two simple Filipino men trying to earn a living." He gave a cynical, threatening smile. "Now, sir, I think you should calm down if you want your wife to leave this car in one piece."

The Englishman slumped back, muttering, "Bloody bastards." He was aware the threat to his lovely young wife was a very serious one.

The remainder of the journey was spent in an uneasy silence, broken only by the steady swish of the windscreen wipers sweeping aside the rivulets of rain streaming down the windows. All the while, the anxious young woman held tightly onto her husband's arm in an effort to calm him.

As the car pulled up outside the tower block containing the British Embassy, Giuseppe looked expectantly at the Englishman, who was by now, understandably, wearing a very sour expression.

The two partners in crime were well used to extreme reactions to their threats. Occasionally, they'd had to use a little violence to persuade their victims to meet their demands, but they'd never yet had to resort to using their gun.

With great reluctance, the Englishman took out his wallet and counted 2,200 pesos—about £60. He handed the wad of notes to Giuseppe, who eagerly took the money and, true to his untrusting nature, slowly and deliberately counted it himself.

"Thank you very much, sir. Would you like us to call back to take you to the airport?"

"You must be bloody crazy!"

That was the usual reaction, not surprisingly, but Giuseppe was unperturbed. He enjoyed this game of 'cat and mouse' and derived great pleasure from goading their victims.

Feeling satisfied with this fare, which was at least ten times the normal rate, Alfredo casually pressed the buttons to release the locking mechanism on the doors. "Enjoy your stay in the Philippines, sir."

With noticeable relief, the man and his bride hurriedly left the car and slammed the door shut.

Alfredo and Giuseppe both laughed loudly as yet another unwitting victim had fallen prey to their enterprising scheme—a scheme which they, and many others like them, had been running for several years, earning them a tidy sum. In such a poor country, everybody struggled for survival, a situation which inevitably breeds violence.

They each lit a cigarette and decided to wait a few minutes in the hope of picking up another fare, preferably back to the airport.

***

Meanwhile, the Englishman and his Filipino wife were inside the embassy, taking the lift to the fifteenth floor, which was one of the floors occupied by the British Consular staff. They were always busy with a steady flow of British men of widely varying ages wishing to marry women from the Philippines. All hopefuls had to go there for authentication of their Certificates of No Impediment prior to getting married.

It was also the place where Filipino brides came for interviews with British Consular staff who had the power to either issue or refuse British residential visas. Sadly, there were many Filipino women who, although being married, were not allowed to join their husbands in Britain. It was quite common to see these beautiful young women heartbroken and in tears at the news of their unsuccessful applications.

***

After a few minutes' wait, with no potential passengers in sight, Alfredo and Giuseppe decided to drive back towards the airport. Alfredo turned the ignition key, slipped into first gear and once again joined the stream of traffic.

They had only driven a short distance when Giuseppe noticed something lying on the rear seat. He laughed loudly. "She was in such a hurry, the stupid woman dropped her bag. I hope she's left some money in it."

As he reached between the seats to pick it up, without warning, the bag burst into bright, orange flames. It burnt with such ferocity that the white nylon seat covers immediately ignited.

Fearing for his life, Alfredo slammed his foot hard on the brake. With a screech of tyres, the car slewed sideways as the vehicle behind them crashed into them.

In a country where seat belts were seldom worn, such an impact had the effect of hurling Alfredo's head hard against the steering wheel, knocking him unconscious. His head jerked back again, and blood from the lacerations on his face dripped onto his shirt, creating a spreading crimson patch.

The front nearside of the car collided with a parked van, compressing the white car like a concertina and jamming the door firmly shut.

In a daze, Giuseppe struggled in vain with his door. With time fast running out as smoke filled the car, he leaned over his partner's limp body, forced the door open, pushed Alfredo out and hastily followed. He collapsed on the ground, retching and coughing from the effects of inhaling the smoke, but relieved to have escaped from the car.

They were still not out of danger, as the two men were in the middle of the road with traffic streaming past, other drivers seemingly oblivious to their plight. Alfredo had barely returned to his senses as Giuseppe dragged him over to the side of the road.

They stared blankly at the huge blisters bubbled over the once-immaculate, now fiercely burning car. Drivers of nearby vehicles braked hard and, together with their passengers, quickly fled on foot as the full realisation of the danger hit them. A second later, an ear-splitting explosion ripped through the air when the fire reached the fuel tank.

Alfredo openly wept as his prized possession was consumed by a brilliant ball of flames. A huge, acrid cloud of black smoke hung over them, eclipsing the sun.

To add to their misery, their earnings from extortionate taxi fares had been concealed in a specially made lining in the glove compartment. In a country where car insurance was the exception rather than the rule, the partners in crime stood little to no chance of recovering anything.

***

On the fifteenth floor of the British Embassy, another woman had joined the couple who, only minutes earlier, had been travelling in the car which was now destroyed.

The Englishman peeled off his moustache and eased the grey wig from his head. His naturally black hair and clean-shaven appearance made him look much younger. A disguise had been necessary to avoid being recognised, and his wife's sister had generously offered to take her place. After being 'stung' by Alfredo and Giuseppe twelve months earlier, he and his wife had vowed vengeance. It was so important that their act be convincing to give them a chance to leave the shoulder bag, carrying the small incendiary device, in the car.

Taking a pair of binoculars, the Englishman scanned the surrounding area. "Look, there!" He pointed excitedly as a cloud of smoke rose steadily between a group of nearby office blocks. Smiles of satisfaction lit all three faces at the confirmation their carefully worked-out plan had succeeded.

No Time for Kate

(August 1994)

Note from the author: In 1994, when my wife and I were living in Midrecht in the Netherlands, I had more ideas for short stories and with permission used my former secretary's name in this story of hope and hopelessness.

***

K ATE WAS WAITING impatiently. Sitting in the darkness of her living room, listening for the sound of the key turning in the door, she was too angry to feel sleepy despite how slowly the time passed by. Eleven o'clock, twelve, one...it was one twenty before she heard the sound she'd been waiting for. She could tell, by the amount of fumbling with the key, how much her husband had drunk: he was having difficulty just finding the door.

Becoming even more irritated by his inept attempts, she was tempted to let him in, yet controlled herself.

After much cursing, Frank pushed the door open and almost fell flat on his face. "Oops, shteady. Musht be quiet. Mushn't wake my boo...boo...bootiful wife. Phew, what a night! What a night!" He made an exaggerated, though unsuccessful attempt at closing the door quietly.

"I know…I know, I'll undresh down here and creep quietly upshtairs. Mushtn't wake Kate."

Kate watched in tempered amusement as her drunken husband, who hadn't thought to switch on the light, dropped his clothes in untidy heaps and staggered around the room, somehow miraculously missing her.

When he was naked and about to sneak up the stairs, she crept up behind him and swiftly grabbed hold of his testicles. In a loud, commanding voice, she ordered, "Don't you dare move, Frank Dobson, or I'll squeeze so hard it'll bring more than tears to your eyes. I might even let you find out what Mr. Bobbit felt like."

"K…K…Kate! Er…hello love. Oh, don't! You're hurting!" The attack had sobered him up far quicker than any other method. "Please let go! What do you want?"

"What do *I* want? What the bloody hell do you think I want, you miserable, drunken slob? If your paunch gets any bigger, you won't need a bloody table to eat your meals on. You wear your old clothes all the time and go for days without shaving. You really are disgusting!

"What I would like is a man who shows me love and tenderness, not one who thinks foreplay is three hours at the pub getting tanked up. I don't think Desmond Morris could include you in his *Mankind* series, unless you were the primitive he was comparing to man." She gave an extra-hard squeeze, causing him to let out an anguished cry, before releasing her hold to switch on the lights.

"My God! Just look at you! The original naked ape! I must have been crazy to marry you, you worthless pig!"

"You have such a wonderful way with words, darling. Listen, I'm tired and dying for a pee. Let's just go to bed, eh?"

"Not bloody likely! You're not sleeping with me in that state. You've done this too many times to get away with it again. You belch and fart all night and couldn't care less if I can't sleep. And then there's your snoring. When you've been drinking, it's like a pneumatic drill in a deep puddle."

"I can't help snoring, you know that."

"But you *can* help getting pissed! For a man who hasn't had a job for two years, you have an uncanny talent for pouring your dole money down the toilet! If I didn't have a decent job, we'd really be in the shit! Right. Now listen to me. Tonight, you are not, I repeat, NOT sleeping with me in that awful state. The only company you'll have tonight is the cat. You can sleep down here on the sofa."

"Oh, Kate, no." Frank appealed pathetically to his wife. "Not the sofa."

"Oh, Kate, yes. I'm absolutely sick of you going with your mates every Friday night, spending money you don't have and then crawling home at all hours in a drunken stupor. I've had enough, do you hear? Enough!"

With that, she stomped upstairs, slamming the bedroom door behind her and leaving Frank, still naked, lost for words.

Muttering curses under his breath, he pulled some of his clothes back on, to try to keep warm during his enforced stay on the sofa. He had never seen his wife so angry before and dared not ask her for bedding, but much to his relief, the bedroom door opened briefly and a pillow and blankets were thrown downstairs. Frank tottered up to the bathroom, where he urgently relieved himself, then nearly fell down the stairs on his way back to the living room. This was not going to be a comfortable night, but it would prove to be a memorable one.

***

It was Kate who woke up first after a restless night— the first one sleeping apart in their twenty-year marriage. Through heavy eyes, she looked at the bedside clock and sat up quickly. "Eleven o'clock! How on earth have I slept so late? That's his fault for keeping me awake half the night."

In haste, she washed, dressed and went downstairs, only to be greeted by the sound of Frank's deep, rumbling snores. She ignored him and went straight to their small kitchen, where she switched on the radio and deliberately turned the volume up, hoping to disturb her slumbering husband. Brian Mathew's warm tones introduced *Sounds of the Sixties*.

She made two mugs of coffee and took one to Frank.

"Come on, you dozy pig. Wake up. I've got some coffee for you."

Frank turned over in an attempt to ignore her calls, but she was insistent. "Please don't shout so loudly. I've a terrible head."

"It serves you bloody well right. You've only got what you deserve. Now come on. Take this coffee from me."

"What time is it?" Frank asked sleepily.

"About eleven fifteen. I don't know how I slept so late, but it's time you were up."

"It can't be that time. That's Brian Mathews on the radio, and his programme finishes at ten. You must have made a mistake."

Kate thought for a few seconds. "You're right. It should be Judy Spires at this time. The clock on the hi-fi—what does that say?" Without waiting for Frank to answer, she looked herself. "It's only eight twenty!"

"You stupid woman! What are you doing waking me up at this time?"

Kate was lost for words. "I don't understand." She rushed upstairs to check the bedside clock and quickly returned. "It definitely says eleven twenty."

"It must have stopped last night."

"Don't be stupid. It was after one thirty when I went to bed, and it was eleven a.m. when I woke up. If you don't believe me, go and have a look for yourself."

She followed Frank upstairs. "See! The clock's still working."

Frank picked up the clock and shook it, as though this might correct it. "That's very strange." He looked around the room and had an inspiration. "Switch on the television and see what's on. I'll go downstairs and switch the other set on."

As he called to Kate from the living room and instructed her to switch over the different channels, it soon became obvious the programmes were not the same.

Frank returned to the bedroom. "There must be a rational explanation for this."

"Oh, yes? And what is that, Mr. Smart-arse?" she asked acidly.

"I don't bloody well know," admitted Frank. "Something in this room has made it go into the future. Somehow, it's three hours ahead of the rest of the world."

"Of course! That's it. And pigs fly, do they?"

"It's the only possible explanation, you know that, but you don't want to admit it, do you? It must be a time warp…or something like that."

"I suppose Doctor Who is going to step out of the wardrobe at any minute."

"Why can't you have an open mind? People used to think the world was flat, until they were proved wrong. Just think of the benefits."

"What benefits? Name me one advantage of having one room three hours ahead of all the others." She could think of none.

"We can make ourselves very rich," Frank said.

"How? Sell our story to the *Sunday Sport*?"

Frank was smiling now. "No, something much easier. If this is real, we could tell which horses are going to win and place bets on them."

"Frank! This is the craziest…" Kate paused and backtracked as she realised what he was saying. "The craziest but the best idea you've had in twenty years. How much do you think we could win?"

"It depends on the odds, but if we place an accumulator, then the winnings of one race are placed on the next, and it could be many thousands of pounds."

Kate's eyes lit up at the thought of it. "This could be the answer to all our dreams. Just promise me one thing, Frank."

"What's that? Send your mother on a world cruise, so she isn't always coming round here?"

"No, you fool. Promise me you won't waste it on drink. If you do, I'll leave you. And I'm not joking."

A look of apprehension crossed his face. "I promise, love. The sofa wasn't very good as a bed. I don't want any more nights like that. Now, the races won't start until after two, so let's go and get some breakfast. I'm starving."

***

"What would you do," Frank asked. "If we had plenty of money, love?"

"What would I do? Oh, there are so many things, I don't know where to start. I'd like to move from this shoebox of a terrace to a detached house. It doesn't have to be a big one. I just want to live without hearing my neighbours screwing all night long. A nice but not too big garden. I could do with a new set of clothes, too. Perhaps a good holiday—I've always wanted to go to Singapore. How about you, Frank? What would you really like?"

"A new car would be definite. But I don't want a Porsche or anything fancy like that. A SAAB 900 would do me nicely. That and a good holiday would be my first choices. I'd like to go to America and see the Space Centre and EPCOT—oh, and the Everglades."

Kate and Frank talked at length about their potential wealth and what they would do with it.

Shortly before eleven, they returned to the bedroom, armed with pen and paper.

They sat on the bed to watch the horse racing, cheering on the horses with high odds. Frank made a note of each winner's name, the odds and the racecourse.

"Right, here's what we're going to do. We'll put a hundred pounds, plus tax, to win accumulator on 'In Love Again', which wins at five-to-one in the two o'clock at Sandown. Next, 'Manssal', at eleven-to-two in the two thirty-five, again at Sandown." He paused, looking through the list of winners. "And we must do this one. 'Ingozi' at twenty-to-one in the three ten. Just one more, I think. Yes, this one. 'Keen Vision' at sixteen-to-one in the four fifteen."

"How much will that all come to?" Kate was excited at the prospect of becoming wealthy.

Frank made some calculations and victoriously exclaimed, "One million, four hundred and fifty-eight thousand, six hundred pounds!"

Kate let out a shriek of delight at this vast amount of money which soon would be theirs. "Oh, Frank, that would be fantastic. We could get everything we ever wanted."

"I still have to place the bets. Let's go downstairs and I'll phone the bookie's." The couple, happier than they had been for a long time, hugged each other and went into their living room.

"Can you place your bets over the phone?"

"As long as I pay by credit card, no problem. Can you look in the directory for the number, love?"

Very soon, they were excitedly dialling the number.

"Hello, I'd like to place some bets on this afternoon's races, please. My name? It's Dobson. Frank Dobson.

Shall I give you my credit card number first? Okay." Frank gave the details. "Now my bets. I want to place a £100, plus tax, to win accumulator on the following horses. First, 'In Love Again' in the two o'clock at Sandown." Frank paused. "What do you mean, it isn't racing? It has to be.

"Well, let's try the next one. 'Manssal' in the two thirty-five at Sandown." Again, another pause and an answer which put a look of puzzlement on Frank's face. "What about 'Ingozi' in the three ten at Sandown?"

His manner was now becoming more anxious, and Kate knew something was very wrong. "I don't understand. All these ran, er, I mean should be running this afternoon. Are you certain? All of them? Just forget it, then. I…I must have made a mistake."

Frank's face had turned ashen as he slowly replaced the receiver.

"What happened?" Kate asked. "Frank? Why could you not place the bets? Tell me, for God's sake!"

"The horses did win. But…they all won yesterday. Just our bloody luck! The time warp in the bedroom isn't three hours ahead. its twenty-one hours behind!"

A Divine Love

(August 1996)

Note from the author: This story tells of the adoration of a well-known pop hero.

***

T HE NOISE WAS deafening, the atmosphere electric and the crowds ecstatic as Michael Jackson appeared through the stage mist. To eighteen-year-old Karen Richards, it was a dream come true. From the age of three, she had followed the career and music of the legendary megastar. She had all his albums and played them incessantly, much to her parents' frustration. Now she was as close to him as the security fencing would allow. When she'd heard Michael was due to give a live concert in her home town of Manchester in May 1988, she was determined to do everything possible to get a front-row seat. Her parents were worried about letting her go, but knew it was pointless to refuse and, instead, had decided to go with her. Karen had never been interested in boyfriends, preferring instead to dream of being with Michael.

Oblivious to the forty thousand other fans filling the grounds at Old Trafford, Karen watched with tears of joy streaming down her cheeks as the man whose pictures adorned her bedroom walls sang for her alone. The whole event was overwhelming as Michael Jackson danced and sang through his vast musical repertoire, never once letting his standards of excellence diminish. By the time he came to perform 'Earth Song', Karen was hoarse from shouting and screaming at her idol.

It was during the powerful, yet moving 'Lost Oceans', his latest hit, that the accident happened. There had been a lot of pushing from the fans who were not so fortunate to be on the front row, but now the pressure had built up to an uncontrollable frenzy. Sue and David Richards looked on in helpless horror as the pressure became intolerable.

Security guards moved in to prevent any casualties, but for Karen, it was too late. About ten girls fell forward, pinning her to the ground, their collective weight crushing her against the fencing. St. John's Ambulance workers, together with the security guards, pulled the screaming girls off and carried them away to tend to their injuries.

Karen's seemingly lifeless body lay in a crumpled heap, her long, black hair covering her face. Sue was crying uncontrollably as David, ignoring the pleas by the medical attendants, lifted his daughter's limp body and cradled her head in his hands.

"Oh, please, Karen, please don't die!"

Eventually, he was persuaded to let them give her proper medical attention, but he insisted on carrying the teenager to a waiting ambulance. During all the panic, Michael Jackson had stopped his performance and pleaded with the audience for some restraint. When he was satisfied that the crowd was more controlled, he continued singing but cast a worried look in Karen's direction.

At the hospital, Karen was given emergency treatment, her anxious parents waiting for news of her condition. Fearing the worst, they were relieved to find that she had recovered consciousness after an hour. She had several cracked ribs, a broken arm and a lot of superficial bruising. Sue and David were both in tears as they were allowed in to see her. Her breathing was very laboured; one of her lungs had been punctured, and she was soon transferred into the capable hands of the Intensive Treatment Unit team, though her parents were never far from her side.

***

Karen kept drifting in and out of sleep, the desire to stay awake sometimes overcoming the effects of the painkilling drugs. She reached out for a drink with a shaky hand, hoping to relieve the awful, parched taste in her mouth, as a nurse entered.

"Do you feel up to having a visitor, Karen?"

Pulling herself up a little, she nodded. A slight figure entered the room.

"You can stay for just a few minutes," the nurse advised. "Miss Richards is very tired."

"Of, course." The figure noticed Karen's outstretched hand, trying to reach her glass.

"Here, please let me help, Karen." He took the glass and held it to her dry lips. Sipping gently, she thought she must be dreaming. The man standing before her, even without his make-up and stage clothes, was unmistakably Michael Jackson. He was so gentle and tender, Karen felt warm and comforted by his presence. "I'm sorry about the accident—I feel responsible."

"Oh, please, Michael, don't be sorry. It wasn't your fault. You don't know how much this means to me. I…I never thought I would meet you. I am so happy!"

The two chatted for several minutes, Michael Jackson, the showman, being replaced by a normal, polite and warm-hearted individual. He signed an autograph for her, and both felt saddened when the nurse returned, ending their private meeting.

"If you don't mind, Mr. Jackson, Miss Richards should get some rest now."

"Michael, will you do one thing for me before you leave?" Karen asked, a rush of colour blushing her cheeks.

"Yes, of course. What is it?"

"Please kiss me, on my lips." She was embarrassed to ask but knew this was the only opportunity she would ever have. The nurse retreated to a discreet position as Michael leaned over and kissed Karen gently yet with so much feeling it overwhelmed her. Tears of happiness ran down her cheeks as he squeezed her hand affectionately.

"I shall remember this moment until the day I die."

"Goodbye, Karen. Take good care of yourself and get better soon." He took a paper out of his pocket and quickly scribbled an address on it. "Write to me and let me know when you are recovered."

Following the nurse, he waved to Karen and disappeared out of sight.

Elated, Karen sank back into her pillow and soon fell into a contented sleep, waking eventually to find her parents sitting at her bedside. Remembering her unexpected visitor, she wondered if it had been a dream and looked on her locker.

"Mum! Dad! Michael Jackson came to see me!" She was so excited she had difficulty getting the words out fast enough.

"Michael Jackson? Here?" Sue asked incredulously.

"Look—here's his autograph. And he's given me his address. He asked me to write to him. Oh, he's so wonderful!" She sighed at the memory of his kiss. "I don't care what the papers say about him. I think he is the warmest, most gentle person I have ever met."

However surprised Karen's parents were, they were thankful this meeting may help to speed up Karen's recovery. It was certainly good to see the joy and happiness in her face, and it stayed throughout the day as Karen underwent many tests to check the condition of her internal organs, which had suffered in the crush.

Later that evening, Karen was watching television in her room. She wasn't really concentrating on the programme, her thoughts occupied with the papers on which her idol had written, until the programme was interrupted for a newsflash.

"Reports are coming in that Michael Jackson, during his performance at Birmingham's NEC, has collapsed on stage, after suffering a major heart attack. He has been rushed to hospital, where his condition is said to be critical."

Karen let out an agonising scream. A nurse quickly appeared, thinking that she was in great pain. She was, but it was of an emotional nature. Karen kept on repeating, "Oh, Michael, please don't die!" and was so upset the nurse had to give her a sedative before she was able to calm down.

Over the days that followed, Karen watched every single news report. She wished she could visit him but knew it was impossible. Unlike Michael's visit to her, massive security would surround the hospital, keeping fans and hungry media at bay.

Apparently, his heart had been badly damaged, and he was being kept alive only by artificial means. There was a lot of speculation in the media about what should be done to save the superstar. There was the possibility of being fitted with a pacemaker, but it was felt that his heart was too badly damaged to sustain life in this way.

A heart transplant was the ideal solution, but for this to be successful, a perfect blood and tissue match was essential. Searches were made of hospitals and transplant lists throughout the world to find a terminally ill patient whose heart could be used, but to no avail.

The media was full of Michael Jackson, exhausting every fact and fiction that had ever been told of his life.

It came as a surprise when Karen learned, from the nurse attending her, that she had the same blood group as Michael, but of course, the chances of a tissue match were phenomenal. She pleaded with the nursing staff to send a sample of her blood for tissue typing but met with much resistance. As they pointed out, it would be a wasted exercise, as she, fortunately, was not in a position to donate her heart.

Although still weak from her injuries, she was making steady progress. Eventually, to keep her quiet, the senior consultant surgeon in charge of Karen's case agreed to a blood sample being taken. He felt certain, once this had been done, that would be the end of the matter.

It came as a shock to everyone when the results showed that her blood and tissue type matched Michael's exactly.

From this point, Karen was a firm believer in fate and pre-determined destiny. She had never been particularly religious, preferring instead to believe what could be proven, yet now she believed everything that happened, however seemingly trivial, was part of the blueprint of the miracle of mankind. She was convinced her accident and meeting with Michael were intricate pieces of a vast jigsaw.

Her parents and the hospital staff noticed a marked difference in Karen after that day. She was calmer, almost serene in manner. Worryingly, her physical condition rapidly deteriorated, and within two days, she was back in Intensive Care.

The consultant surgeon had to admit to Sue and David that he was puzzled by Karen's condition. "She had been making such good progress that this relapse is completely inexplicable. But don't worry, we will do everything possible to treat your daughter."

Those were brave words, and it was soon clear that even he was powerless to stop the decline. Sue and David kept a vigil at Karen's bedside. Another twenty-four hours passed, and the remaining life in Karen's body was only being sustained by mechanical means.

The consultant had to admit defeat. "I have seen many cases of people giving up the will to live, but never have I seen anyone positively wish to die. In one of her few moments of consciousness, your daughter begged us to let her die and to give her heart to Michael Jackson. In the circumstances, I feel this is the only option left, but I need your permission before I cease treatment."

Sue and David knew it was what Karen really wanted and, reluctantly, agreed to the surgeon's request. From there, events moved swiftly. The hospital in which Michael Jackson was being treated was informed and a transport successfully completed: within two days of the operation, Michael's condition improved rapidly.

Sitting up in his hospital bed, he opened an envelope which Karen had asked to be given to him. The writing was shaky and barely legible, but the message was clear. Tears ran down Michael Jackson's face as he read:

> *To thee, my heart I give,*
> *In order that you may live,*
> *for no other love but mine,*
> *can make this sacrifice so divine.*

74

Janet and John at the Hospital

(2017)

Note from the author: I have always been a strong fan of Sir Terry Wogan, listening to his programmes on BBC Radio 2. His 'Janet and John' stories are legendary, and I hope the BBC do not mind me using these characters for my short story collection. My tribute also goes to the writer of Terry's sketches, a talented listener who went under the name Mick Sturbs.

***

AFTER MANY YEARS of raised blood pressure caused by John's antics, Janet needed to see the consultant at the hospital heart unit for a check-up.

As she was called into the consulting room, she said to John, "Just wait for me here and don't get into any trouble."

"I won't," said John as he settled in the comfortable seat.

After a few minutes, Miss Frobisher walked into the area and saw John, playing with the tassels on his suit and looking rather bored.

"Hello, John. What are you doing, here?"

"Oh, I'm waiting for Janet. She's with the consultant."

Miss Frobisher looked thoughtful. "John, could you help me? I've had a cancellation, and I need to recalibrate the echo-cardiogram system. It won't take very long. Would you like to help?"

"Yes, of course!" John skipped happily as Miss Frobisher led the way to her laboratory.

"I'll need you to take off your top, John," she said, adding, "Here, let me help," when he struggled to unfasten the ties on his suit. With her nimble fingers, John's silk top and knitted woollen vest were soon removed. See John shiver.

"Please lie down on this bed, and then I can prepare you." John's eyes grew wide as he allowed Miss Frobisher to apply very messy jelly to his chest. "This jelly makes the job easier."

"Ooh, it's very cold and it tickles."

Miss Frobisher ran the probe over John's chest while watching the screen. "My, that's quick, John. I found the spot straight away. Just see your heart beating." She turned the monitor to give him a good view. As she increased the speaker volume, he could both see and hear his heartbeat.

After a few minutes, Miss Frobisher said, "John, do you think you could turn onto your left side and raise your hand above your head?"

"Yes, of course." He did as she requested, allowing her to run the probe up near his armpit.

"Perfect! Thank you so much, John. You have been a great help. Here, use this tissue to clean the jelly off." She assisted him in wiping the mess off his chest before he put his vest and top back on and skipped happily back to the waiting room.

"Where have you been?" asked Janet, rather sternly. "I told you to wait here."

"Oh, Miss Frobisher asked me if she could have me for a quickie. She took off my clothes and covered me with jelly. She said it would make it better and was surprised when we found the spot so quickly. My heart was pounding so fast I could hear it clearly while she probed me for best contact. Then she decided to try me in a different position and asked me to put my hand up. She was really pleased with the results and thanked me for helping her. I did get a stain on my clothes, but she said it would soon disappear."

Do you know how far a clinical thermometer can be pushed up John's rectum? Janet does!!

Janet and John at the Shopping Centre

(2017)

Note from the author: Here is another Janet and John story to keep you smiling.

***

WHEN JANET AND John entered the shopping mall, Janet said, in her usual stern voice, "Right, John. I'm going to be a while in the ladies' stores, looking for a new dress. You can look around the mall, but I want you back here outside Selfridges at four o'clock. Have you got your watch on?"

John looked down at his Timex Roy Rogers wristwatch, Roy's gun hand moving as every second passed. "Yes, Janet. I'll be here at four."

"And don't get into any trouble."

"I won't." John skipped happily through the crowds, looking resplendent in his silk yellow shirt with ruffles and bell-bottomed green corduroy trousers. See John's beaming face at the chance of looking around the shops on his own. He had plenty of time.

John decided to use the escalator to go to the first floor, where there were many of his type of shops. He knew the rules about standing on the right to let people pass on the left if they were in a hurry.

As John stepped on the escalator, he noticed Miss Peacock, the kind lady from the local haberdashers, standing in front of him.

"Hello, Miss Peacock," John said politely.

She turned around and recognised him immediately. "Why, hello, John. What are you doing here?"

"Oh, I'm just looking around the shops while Janet is shopping for a new dress."

They continued chatting and were nearly at the top of the escalator when John's trouser bottom became wedged in the mechanism. Face flushed, he tugged hard to free his trousers and, with a tremendous effort, managed to pull them free.

As he did so, he overbalanced and fell on to Miss Peacock, yet she managed to avoid falling. Realising John's misfortune, she helped him to his feet. "Are you all right, John?" She hoped he had not injured himself.

He looked down and noticed a small rip in his trousers where he had tugged himself free from the escalator. See John blub!

Miss Peacock looked concerned. "Don't worry, John. I always have needle and thread in my bag, ready for any emergency, so I can soon fix that small tear for you."

John wiped the tears from his eyes and thanked her.

"Let's find somewhere quiet to sit while I repair your trousers."

Soon, they were sitting down, John wrapped in a plastic raincoat while Miss Peacock stitched the tear in his pants, making a very professional job, the tear now hardly visible.

After thanking her, he looked at his watch and realised he was going to be late meeting Janet. See John rush through the crowds!

Janet was angry. "Where have you been?" she demanded.

"Oh, I saw Miss Peacock while I was going up the escalator. She was very pleased to see me, and before I knew what was happening, I felt a tug on my pants. After finding a quiet place for us, she gave me a plastic mac for protection, telling me that she always had one in her bag, just in case. She was very quick, and with her nimble fingers had soon made me feel much happier.

Do you know how to squeeze someone into a shopping centre waste bin? Janet does.

Help Me, Rhonda!

(2013, 2017)

Note from the author: This story was originally a script for a sit-com TV series. Unfortunately, the BBC did not accept it, so I rewrote it in 2017 as a short story.

Chapter One:
Difficult Times

THE ELDERLY COUPLE, Harry and Emma Dale, lived in their small, ground-floor apartment on the outskirts of Liverpool, having moved there four years ago from the semi-detached council house where they had lived for over forty years. With their increasing infirmity, the new apartment was supposed to make life easier, removing the need to climb the stairs many times each day.

Seventy-five-year-old Emma Dale leaned her walking stick against the kitchen unit as she reached up to open the so-called eye-level cupboard. Even standing on her toes, she was unable to touch the bottle.

"Why are these cupboards so high here?" she grumbled to herself. The sound of loud cheering could be heard from the television in the living room, where her seventy-eight-year-old husband was watching football. "Harry! Can you give me a hand, please?"

"What do you want?" he asked irritably.

"I need your help to reach a bottle for me, please."

Harry's reply, spoken in his strong, Scouse accent, was not particularly helpful. "Can't you wait a minute? They're about to take a penalty!"

"If you want some dinner tonight, you'd better be quick, penalty or not!"

Harry, annoyed by her persistence, walked stiffly into the kitchen. "What is it?"

Emma pointed to the bottle in the cupboard. "That's the one. It's a sauce I want to use in a casserole."

Her rattled husband stared up at the bottle. "Why did you put it up so bloody high?" He reached for it, but before he could grab it, a sharp, arthritic pain caused him to collapse on the floor. "Oh, shit! My bloody back!"

Emma hurried over to her husband. "Oh, Harry! Are you all right?"

"Do I bloody well look all right? It's this damn rheumatism and arthritis." Seeing her concern, Harry softened a little. "Give me a hand up, please, love. I think we may have to manage without that sauce in our casserole."

With their combined effort, they managed to get him seated on a kitchen chair, each little movement making him flinch.

Emma used her mobile phone to contact the surgery and requested a home visit; within a couple of hours, the doctor was sitting in the Dales' living room.

Doctor Victoria Thompson was a good-looking woman with a pleasant disposition, in her early forties, although her long, black hair made her look a few years younger. She scanned through her notes, checking the recorded details of her patient.

Harry, impatient as ever, asked, "Are you sure there is nothing you can do for me, Doctor?"

In no hurry, she finished her reading and lifted her head. "Not really. You're on the best medication for your type of rheumatoid arthritis. Apart from keeping up with that, there's nothing else we can do. Gentle exercise is important, so try to avoid staying in one position for any length of time."

"He does sit for hours watching television," Emma said, "but it's difficult for both of us. We both have arthritis, and every day is a struggle to live as normally as possible."

Doctor Thompson listened sympathetically. "I do understand. Have you ever considered getting home assistance?"

Harry bristled with indignation at this suggestion. "Absolutely not! I've heard many stories of these home carers only being allowed thirty minutes to get a person showered, dressed and give them breakfast. It would take nearly that long for me just to have a crap!" Emma and the Doctor looked at each other with some discomfort. "Two or even three short visits a day are just no bloody good."

All three of them startled when the front door opened and the Dales' son and daughter-in-law walked in.

"Sorry to interrupt," Alan, their son, said. "We came as quickly as we could. How's Dad?"

"It's okay. I've just about finished, now. All your father can do is to take things easy."

"That's not difficult," Alan remarked sardonically. "He only breaks into a sweat when his favourite striker misses a goal!"

"That's not fair, Alan," Emma interjected. "Your father's worked hard on the railway all his life, with hardly any time off sick."

"Until thirteen years ago, when he retired and began a very close relationship with his chair."

The ever-patient doctor ignored the banter. "I'll call again in another three days to keep a check on you, Mr. Dale."

Grateful for her attention, Harry said, "Thanks, Doctor. I'm sorry to be such a pain in the backside."

Alan's wife Lynn escorted Doctor Thompson to the external door and returned to the living room.

"So, how are you really feeling, Dad?" Alan asked.

"A bit pissed off. I could do with a body transplant. Why did nobody tell me sixty-odd years ago, that when you're old, the body mechanism seizes up?"

Taking a seat, Alan said, "Listen, Dad. Did you know there's a new retirement home only about four miles from here?"

"No, Alan, I didn't know that, and to be absolutely honest, I couldn't give a shit! It might as well be a thousand miles away for all the hope you've got of getting us into one of them places."

Lynn came back into the room and, ignoring her father-in-law's hostility, added, "They can give you great peace of mind with all the support you get in these homes, you know."

"You mean it would give *the both of you* peace of mind if we were shunted into one of those death farms!"

"Calm down, love," Emma beseeched. "You need to keep your blood pressure under control."

"My blood pressure is fine, thanks, but I'll tell you this. When I leave this flat, it'll be in a coffin!"

In a quiet voice, Alan retorted, "I'm certain that could be arranged."

Lynn shot an angry look at her husband. "There must be a solution to this problem, Dad. Leave it with me and I'll see what I can come up with."

Chapter Two:
An Introduction to Rhonda

FOLLOWING LYNN'S ENQUIRIES, a social worker, Angela, visited Harry and Emma. She referred to her notes. "You look well for your age, Mr. Dale. I thought you were in your late sixties, but I see from your record that you're seventy-eight."

Harry was pleased by her observations. "Right now, I'm feeling crap and definitely my age." After a moment's thought, he added with a cheeky smile, "Sometimes I feel like a twenty-five-year-old, but Emma won't let me!"

Angela ignored this flippant remark. "I'm sorry, Mr. and Mrs. Dale, but the plain truth is, both of you could do with some assistance to help you get through the day. Now, I could organise a home carer to call on you, say three times a day—"

"You can forget that! I don't want someone coming round here for a few minutes and creating havoc. I prefer our own mess to one created by a so-called helper!"

Unfazed by Harry's hostility to her suggestion, Angela said, "I'm sorry you feel that way. I know you don't like the idea of a retirement home, but how about a full-time carer? Would that help to change your mind?"

"Wouldn't that be very expensive?" asked Emma, convinced their pensions would not be sufficient for a full-time carer. "I thought the council was looking for ways to reduce the social welfare costs?"

Angela smiled at Emma's understandable concern. "It would be expensive if it was a human being, but I was thinking of a robot."

"Robot?" Harry spluttered. "You can't be serious! Surely, they can't be that sophisticated, can they?"

"There's a new generation of lower-cost, domestic robots, which I think may be the perfect solution for you."

"Now that sounds a better idea! I'm definitely interested."

"Good! After your son told me you weren't happy about a retirement home, I checked out all the possible alternatives. I think this may be a realistic solution. Leave it with me and I'll organise a demonstration."

***

A week later, Harry was sitting reading a newspaper when the doorbell rang.

Emma slowly got to her feet and went to answer it. She returned with a man following her and offered him a seat.

"Good afternoon," he said, "I'm Dennis." He looked to be in his late thirties and had a noticeably nervous expression. "Thanks for allowing me to come here and show you the benefits of our newly released domestic robot."

"Newly released?" Emma asked anxiously. "I hope it's going to be reliable. Is it from Japan or America?"

"I'm afraid that with the government cuts, we could not afford the expense of Japanese or American technology. But I can assure you each model is extremely reliable and thoroughly tested before it's made available in a domestic situation."

Harry, realising Dennis was holding back on some information, asked, "So where is this robot?"

Dennis gave a nervous laugh. "Oh, just in the hall. If you're ready, I'll call her in." He turned towards the partly open door. "Rhonda! Come here, please."

The door opened fully, and a Filipino-looking woman walked stiffly into the room. If she had been human, she'd have been twenty to thirty years old, about five foot four inches tall, slim and had long, black hair.

Harry's face lit up and his jaw dropped in admiration at the sight of the beautiful young woman standing in front of him. "Good God! She's a looker! Rhonda? What sort of a name is that?"

"Rhonda stands for Robotic, House-Owner's Natural, Domestic Assistant."

"Really? It sounds more like a bloody valley in Wales, to me!"

Dennis turned to the robot. "Introduce yourself, Rhonda."

Rhonda followed Dennis's instructions, speaking in a typically robotic fashion, yet the language was not English; it was Tagalog, a dialect commonly used in the Philippines. "*Kumusta kayo*, Mr. and Mrs. Dale. *Masaya ako na mag alaga sa iyong dalawa.*"

"What the bloody hell is she talking about?" Harry demanded. "Do we have to learn that language?"

Dennis looked distinctly uncomfortable. "Er, no. Sorry, I forgot to change the language to English. She is the very

91

latest technology, direct from Manila." Dennis pointed a remote control at Rhonda and pressed a few buttons.

Rhonda began to speak again. "Hello, Mr. and Mrs. Dale. My name is Rhonda, and I am happy to look after you both."

"That's remarkable," Emma said. "She's very life-like, isn't she, Harry?"

Harry was staring at Rhonda and grinning. "She certainly is. So what can she do?"

"Ask her," Dennis suggested. "She understands everything we say."

"Pleased to meet you, Rhonda. My name is Harry and my wife is Emma. Tell me what you can do for me…er, I mean us."

"Hello, Harry. I can clean the house, cook your meals, assist you with personal hygiene and many other tasks. I can ease the load from Emma to make both your lives easier."

"I bet you can."

Emma gave her husband a look of disapproval.

Dennis explained, "Rhonda's intelligence is intuitive, allowing her to learn and adapt to your particular requirements." He opened his briefcase and removed a thick booklet. He handed this, together with the remote control, to Harry. "Right. I think I can leave Rhonda with you now. Here's the instruction manual in case you encounter any problems."

Harry grimaced as he felt the weight of the manual. "God, it's heavy! I hope it's in English."

Dennis gave a nervous little laugh. "Oh, yes. English is on pages one hundred and eighty-five to three hundred and forty-two." He stood, seeming desperate to escape. "I'll leave you in Rhonda's capable hands."

Keen to try out this new technology, Harry instructed, "Rhonda, show Dennis to the door, please."

Immediately, Rhonda grabbed Dennis roughly by the upper arm, pulling him towards the living room door. "Look, Dennis! This is a door!"

Flustered, Dennis struggled free of Rhonda's tight grip, massaging his bruised arm as he turned back to Harry and Emma. "Please remember Rhonda is a robot and will execute commands literally." Turning to Rhonda, he said, "It's okay, Rhonda. I will let myself out, thank you." Dennis hurriedly left the apartment, slamming the outer door behind him.

Rhonda lifted her eyebrows in an expression emulating annoyance at the disappearing salesman.

Emma, strangely, felt sympathy for the robot. "Rhonda, come and sit down in that chair." Emma pointed to an empty chair, and Rhonda complied. "Now, tell me, what sort of food can you cook for us?"

The smile returned to Rhonda's face. "Many dishes like calamari, adobong baboy or manok, bodbod or apritada."

"Can you cook things a little more British? Like fish and chips, steak pie or a pork casserole?" Concentrating on her question, Emma was unaware that Harry was studying Rhonda's shapely legs.

"I can cook anything. I am connected to the internet and can check recipes from anywhere in the world."

"How about asking her to make beans on toast?" Harry said. "It's simple and nearly lunchtime."

Emma thought this was a reasonable idea. "Okay. Rhonda, we would like you to make beans on toast for us. Come with me, and I'll show you where everything is in the kitchen."

Harry watched Rhonda's shapely figure follow Emma as requested.

In the kitchen, Emma showed Rhonda around the cupboards, indicating which areas she would need for the preparation of lunch. "Now, Rhonda, here is the bread. There is the toaster, and the beans are in that cupboard." Emma pointed. "The plates, knives and forks are in here."

"Okay, Emma. You relax, and I will prepare lunch for you and Harry."

Smiling, Emma returned to the living room.

Seemingly efficient, Rhonda placed two slices of bread in the toaster but did not yet depress the handle to start the toasting process. Opening the cupboard containing the various tins, she removed one and, placing the can at eye level, scanned the label. "Rice pudding, not beans." She replaced the tin in the cupboard and repeated the process until the tin of beans was located.

She opened the tin and poured the contents into a pan, which she placed on the hob. While this was heating up, she retrieved plates and cutlery.

In the living room, Harry and Emma listened to the sounds of Rhonda preparing their meal.

"She seems happy enough," Emma said.

After a few minutes, Rhonda appeared in the doorway, carrying the tray with the plates. "Where do you wish to eat your beans on toast?"

Emma stood and slowly made her way to the dining table. "On here, please, Rhonda." Meanwhile, Harry pressed the button on his large, reclining chair, assisting him to stand upright. He shuffled over to the dining table and took his seat.

Rhonda rested the tray and began to transfer the plates and cutlery to the table. "Have a good meal, Harry and Emma."

"Thanks," said Harry. As he and Emma looked at their plates, both were dumbfounded. "Rhonda? What the bloody hell is this?"

"Beans on toast, as you requested."

"But these are runner beans! They're meant to be baked bloody beans!"

Rhonda retained her smile as she said, "You requested beans on toast. You did not specify baked bloody beans!"

Emma had a resigned look on her face as she said to Harry, "I think this may take a little getting used to."

Rhonda continued smiling, unaware that the meal she had prepared was not to the couple's liking, but with some tuition from Emma, she would eventually overcome the initial problems. They even enjoyed some of the more adventurous meals lifted from the internet by the ever-courteous Rhonda.

Chapter Three:
A Design Flaw

THE FOLLOWING DAY, Harry was, as usual, sitting in his reclining chair, while Emma was tidying some magazines.

"Can I help?" asked Rhonda.

"Yes, please, Rhonda. Harry and I are going for a rest in the bedroom, giving you a chance to dust and vacuum this room without us getting in your way. Come on, Harry."

Harry put down his newspaper and pressed the button on his chair to assist him to stand, but even with the chair's help he was struggling. Harry had a sudden inspiration. "Rhonda! Can you give me a hand, please?"

Rhonda's usual smile was replaced with a puzzled expression. "I'm sorry, Harry, but I do not have a spare hand. You can have my left one if you really need it." To Harry's horror, she began to unscrew her left hand.

"No, Rhonda! I don't want your hand. Either of them. All I want is for you to help me get up out of this chair! Okay?"

Rhonda, still quite calm, screwed her hand back on.

"Sorry, Harry. Let me help you." She stood in front of him, taking hold of his upper arms, and then pulled him into a standing position much faster than he'd expected.

"Good God, Rhonda! You're very strong! I've never stood up so fast! I think I my bloody piles behind in the chair!"

Rhonda studied the empty chair.

Emma chuckled. "Come on, Harry! Let's give Rhonda some space."

The couple walked out of the room, leaving Rhonda to start the cleaning, and as she worked, she talked to herself. "These humans are so strange. Emma said they would give me some space, but where is it?"

Rhonda dusted all horizontal surfaces, removing items one at a time. She accidentally knocked an ornament off the mantelpiece yet deftly caught it and replaced it precisely where it had been standing.

On one wall there was a large mirror, and every time Rhonda passed it, she gave an extra-wide, admiring smile.

After dusting, she plugged the vacuum cleaner into the wall socket and happily sang to herself as she vacuumed the floor, still admiring her reflection in the mirror whenever she passed it.

Noticing a newspaper on the floor where it had fallen off Harry's chair, she bent to retrieve it, but her designers had not perfected this process, and as a result, Rhonda overbalanced. She had no choice but to call for help.

"Harry! Emma! Please assist me! Unable to regain standing position!"

Harry and Emma hurried from the bedroom and looked in amazement at Rhonda lying face down on the floor, her feet scrabbling to gain purchase.

"Rhonda! What the bloody hell happened?"

"Overbalanced trying to pick up newspaper. Please assist!"

The elderly couple, faced with this very unusual situation, stood one on either side of the prone robot, painfully bending to hoist Rhonda by her arms until she could stand on her own.

Harry, exhausted and surprised, said, "God, you're a hell of a weight!"

Emma gave him a sharp look. "Are you all right, now, Rhonda?"

The robot appeared to be doing some self-testing, as she delayed before she answered, "I think so. Will carry out a recalibration." Her expression went blank, and at one stage her eyes appeared to cross. After about twenty seconds, her smile returned. "Everything checks okay. Sorry I had to ask for your assistance."

"Don't worry, Rhonda," Emma said. "It's good to know we're not yet completely useless."

After a moment's thought, Harry said, "If it's a problem to pick up small objects from the floor, you can use my grabber if you want."

"Thank you, Harry."

For the next few minutes, Harry explained how to use the grabbing device, picking up the newspaper several times until the robot mastered use of this handy tool.

Harry showed Rhonda where to find the grabber, should she need it at any time.

Chapter Four:
A Halloween Fright

HARRY AND EMMA were sitting at their dining table. Both were anxious, following their experience of Rhonda's beans on toast the previous day.

The sound of Rhonda's preparations could be heard from the kitchen, the robot singing happily while preparing the food.

Speaking quietly to his wife, Harry said, "I hope she does better today."

Emma smiled. "I think she will. I spent quite a while today showing her where everything is and explaining the meanings behind British dishes. She's also looking on the internet at the various recipes of famous British cooks like Delia Smith, Gary Rhodes and Jamie Oliver."

Harry sniffed the air. "It certainly smells good. Keep your fingers crossed she doesn't put fireworks into the sausages to make them bangers!

Emma rolled her eyes at Harry's feeble joke.

Smiling, Rhonda emerged from the kitchen carrying a tray loaded with dishes. She rested the tray on the table and placed the dishes in front of the elderly couple. "I hope you both enjoy this meal. No misunderstandings?"

Harry tried the sausages and mashed potatoes; a rich, tasty gravy covered the sausages. "Mmmm, this is fantastic! Well done, Rhonda!"

Emma tried some and nodded in agreement.

The couple picked up their glasses of wine and toasted their robot helper.

"Congratulations! You have done a fantastic job!"

Emma could have sworn Rhonda's face blushed at their compliments. Yet how could that be? Surely, a robot could never have such emotions.

After their enjoyable meal, the couple relaxed, watching a wildlife documentary on the television. Surprisingly, Rhonda sat nearby, seeming very interested in the wide array of animals highlighted by David Attenborough.

While the three of them were enjoying the programme, the doorbell rang.

"Who the hell is that?" Harry muttered. "Can you find out who's at the door, Rhonda? If it's kids, scare them off!"

Obediently, Rhonda left the room.

As she opened the front door, Rhonda was confronted by three older children, all dressed in Halloween costumes and giggling at their own horrific images.

"Can I help you?" Rhonda asked.

"Trick or treat?" one of the children said in a spooky voice.

Rhonda was puzzled by this question, but within a fraction of a second, she had scanned her memory bank. "I think I will choose trick. How is this for a trick?" Her head began to revolve until it was spinning so fast her features were a mere blur.

Terrified, the three teenagers ran away screaming.

Satisfied at a job well done, Rhonda checked the alignment of her head and returned to the living room.

"Who was it, Rhonda? What was that scream?"

"I think they were children in costumes. They asked, 'Trick or treat?'"

"What did you do?"

"You told me to scare them. I decided a trick would be appropriate, so I checked my internet data for scary effects and revolved my head a few times. They seemed quite frightened. Did I do it right?"

Harry burst out laughing. "I'm not bloody surprised! That's a fantastic party trick and guaranteed to scare the pants off them. Great work, Rhonda!"

Emma was laughing too. "I don't think those children will return here, ever."

***

The following day, while Harry was relaxing in his chair, reading a paperback and drinking from a mug of hot chocolate, Emma called the social worker.

"Hello, it's Emma Dale. Yes, I'm phoning about Rhonda. It was a bit tricky, at first. She seems to have a lot of Filipina instincts built into her intelligence, but she's adapting to a British way of life and is far better than we could ever have imagined." She paused to listen. "Oh, yes, we would like to keep her, please. She works as hard as five people, and I know it sounds silly, but I'm becoming quite fond of her. Yes, thanks so much. Goodbye."

Emma replaced the receiver as Harry slowly stood and, carrying his mug, walked into the kitchen. Absent-mindedly, he went to the sink to put his mug down.

It was then that he noticed Rhonda standing immobile and erect, facing the wall close to the fridge.

"Rhonda, are you all right?"

As she turned around, a wire could be seen protruding from the place where a human's navel would be. The other end was plugged into a small unit connected to the mains wall socket.

With a look of mild embarrassment, Rhonda replied, "Yes, I am okay, Harry. My battery level was running a bit low, so I took the time to have a trickle charge. I hope you don't mind."

It was now Harry's turn to be embarrassed. "Oh, not at all. Sorry to disturb you. Carry on charging and, by the way, Rhonda, welcome to our little family."

Rhonda again turned to face the wall, smiling to herself, happy to be accepted by Harry and Emma.

A Universal Threat

(2018)

Note from the author: After our family holiday at Universal Studios in Florida, I had this idea for a story. It is not quite long enough for a book on its own yet is a bit lengthy for a short story. I hope you all enjoy it.

Chapter One:
Hard Rock Hotel

THE SLEEK, WHITE taxi came to an abrupt halt in the queue outside the huge, metal entrance gates of the Hard Rock Hotel at Universal Studios in Florida.

"This is quite the line. Are you somebody famous?" the middle-aged taxi driver asked of her British passengers, Paul and Suzanne Kennedy, who were accompanied by their children, Jason and Rebecca.

"I wish!" Paul smiled at her question. If there was anybody famous visiting the hotel, it most certainly was not him, but perhaps in his dreams, he could be coming to the hotel as a famous celebrity.

"I hope they're quick," the driver said. "My next pick-up is at eight."

Paul looked at his watch: it was seven forty-five. She would have difficulty making her appointment. It was then he realised the reason for their delay. "It's the last Thursday in the month. They always have a live band on tonight. I'd forgotten about that."

This did not lessen the taxi driver's obvious anxiety, but thankfully, the cars began to move forward, allowing access to the area in front of the main reception hall.

The British family climbed out of the air-conditioned taxi into the heat of the Florida night. They retrieved their suitcases with the help of their driver. "That will be fifty-seven dollars, please."

The hotel had advised Paul the fare would be around that amount, which he thought to be quite reasonable considering the length of the journey from the airport to the hotel. He declined change from the notes he handed to the driver, who gave him an appreciative smile and climbed back into her car, eager to make her next customer.

Paul and his family pulled their suitcases up the incline into the ornate lobby, only to be met by a tremendous, deafening noise. Several hundred people were gathered in there, all talking excitedly as they waited for the presumably well-known rock group to appear.

The noise was so loud it was difficult to converse with the receptionist, who seemed to be in great demand. Paul handed over a printout of the confirmation email to ease their communication problem. After a few ear-shattering minutes, she handed over four key cards, indicating the direction to the lifts. "You need to insert your room key to access the seventh floor," she shouted, her voice barely audible above the continuous background noise.

The four pulled their cases towards the lift corridor, where Rebecca eagerly pressed the call button. There were six lifts, and soon one of the doors opened, allowing them inside. At last, they could speak without having to shout to be heard.

Jason, a skinny, long-haired fourteen-year-old, asked, "Why do you need the room key for the lift, Dad?"

Paul smiled as he placed it into the slot above the buttons and pressed number seven. "The seventh floor is an exclusive club level, and those with rooms on the lower floors are not allowed."

"Cool!"

Paul had thought his son would appreciate the extra benefits of this club level and was glad that so far it seemed to be worth the extra expense. Jason had been asking him if they could stay in the Hard Rock Hotel for years; after several refusals, Paul decided to give him this treat, along with a few other surprises.

Rock music was playing in the lift, and pictures of stars adorned the walls. A huge mirror covered the whole of the ceiling, giving a somewhat strange visual effect within the confined space.

As they emerged on the seventh floor, they found a welcoming central area with a lounge bar and three corridors leading off. Looking at the wall plates indicating the range of room numbers for each corridor, they determined which way they needed to go.

Suzanne found room 7090 and inserted her key, pushing the heavy door open. The four dragged their cases inside and looked around the spacious place where they would spend the next ten nights. Although they had stayed at Disneyworld several years earlier, this was their first holiday at Universal Studios, and today, Thursday, 27th July 2023, would be a very memorable day.

More pictures of rock legends adorned the walls of their suite, continuing the theme of the hotel. The room they were in was quite large with an impressive king-size bed: this was where Paul and Suzanne would sleep.

Jason noticed the connecting door and pulled it open. "Cool!" This typical teenage response reflected his satisfaction with the twin-bedded room he would share with his younger sister. Each room had its own bathroom, wardrobe and high-definition flatscreen television.

While everyone else was looking around the suite, Suzanne stood near the large window, admiring the view. "Look!" She pointed at a huge structure in the distance.

Paul followed her gaze. "It's Hogwarts! What a fantastic view. I think this is going to be our best holiday ever." If only he could have known!

He pulled his wife close, giving her an affectionate hug and kiss. The couple gazed, almost spellbound, through the window at the panorama before them. It was nearly dusk, and the many colourful lights added to the magic of the world-famous theme park laid out below.

Their gaze over this scene was interrupted by their nine-year-old daughter's cry of, "I'm hungry!"

Paul wasn't surprised. Rebecca had not eaten much on the flight from Manchester, as she had never enjoyed in-flight meals.

"Can we get a snack now, Mummy?"

"Yes. We'll try the lounge bar."

The four left their luggage unpacked and walked back along the corridor. The double glass doors to the lounge were closed, but there was a slot next to them. Paul inserted his room key, and the doors opened automatically.

Snacks and drinks were laid out at one end of the room, and most of the small tables had people sitting around them, chatting noisily. One man was strumming a guitar while talking to a small group of people. The room had a lively, welcoming atmosphere, adding to the attraction of the world-famous hotel.

The Kennedy family helped themselves to savoury snacks and drinks before finding somewhere to sit. They had timed their arrival perfectly, as another family were leaving, making space for them. They took their time with their refreshments, listening to and enjoying the songs of the man with the guitar, who was unknown to them but played some recognisable rock classics to his appreciative audience.

Rebecca, although excited, was really quite tired after her first day of the holiday, and it wasn't long before the Kennedys returned to their room for the night.

Suzanne soon found the children's night clothes, and within a few minutes, Rebecca was climbing into her comfortable bed, chattering excitedly about the next day's visit to the theme park.

Jason, surprisingly, did not yet feel tired and tried to find something of interest on television, knowing that the noise would not stop his sister from falling asleep.

***

As Paul, Suzanne and their children headed out for the quayside the next morning, the humid Florida air engulfed them. With temperatures in the high nineties, the main challenge of the day would be to avoid getting burnt, and with this in mind, Suzanne had covered them all liberally with high-factor sun cream. As they walked down the path, they noticed a gate leading to a small jetty. They were given a typically American friendly greeting by the bearded captain of the water taxi and took their seats towards the back. When most seats were occupied, the ropes were cast off and the cruiser moved slowly through the water.

In less than ten minutes, they had reached the entrance to Universal Theme Park and disembarked. The place was already heaving as they approached the ticket barrier to activate their passes. After a few minutes' wait, Paul handed over the receipt provided by the travel agent to a tall, heavily built guy.

"Can I see your passport, sir?"

Paul handed it to the man, who looked at him and then the picture on the passport. Satisfied that Paul was the same person, he continued in a deep, monotone voice that spoke of how many times he had been through this routine before, "Place your index finger on the reader, sir."

Obediently, Paul pressed it on the glass. Once his finger had been scanned, the other members of his family were similarly scanned and each issued with a fourteen-day park pass.

Within a matter of minutes, the family was poring over a map of Universal Studios, trying to agree on which parts to visit first. They eventually agreed to let Jason and his dad go on the RIP ride, while Suzanne and Rebecca, not feeling brave enough, waited for their return.

As Paul approached the queue, he noticed the alternative express route. "Show your room key and we can get on this ride much quicker."

Jason followed his dad's instruction and was amazed how they were allowed to pass the already lengthy queue and were soon sitting in the ride's car, ready for the thrill of this well-known attraction. It was obvious when the overhead clamp locked into position, that they were going to experience a stomach-churning ride. After slowly climbing up a steep incline, the car raced along at an incredible speed, twisting and turning in all directions. Many of the occupants were screaming as they were subjected to extreme forces as the car completed a full circle, racing upside down and sideways.

When they eventually returned to the station, they disembarked and re-joined Suzanne and Rebecca at the point where photos of every person on the ride were already displayed.

"You look terrified, Jason!" Suzanne laughed at the expression on her son's face. "You looked quite calm, Paul."

"He always is," said Jason enviously. "I don't know how he does it. Dad looks as though he's waiting for a nice cup of tea."

They all laughed, Suzanne finding money to purchase the photograph as a souvenir.

"I'm glad I didn't have a big breakfast this morning," Paul admitted. "My stomach's feeling the effects of all the twists and turns of the ride."

After that, they opted for a more relaxing type of entertainment in Minion Mayhem, one of the many indoor, air-conditioned 4D shows, suitable for all members of the family.

They all agreed to brave Jurassic Park, where all four could sit on one of the five rows in a large boat. At first, it moved sedately through the water, with, supposedly, prehistoric animals lining the banks of what was meant to be a river coursing through a dense jungle. When it entered a huge cavern, the recorded commentary sounded alarms and warnings that carnivorous monsters could endanger the lives of the occupants of the boat.

The excitement increased as the craft picked up speed. In an effort to escape the monsters, it emerged from the blackness of the cave into bright sunlight, dropping eighty feet into water and creating a tremendous splash, which liberally soaked everyone on board. Rebecca and Suzanne were not too enamoured with the ride, but Jason and his dad loved every second.

***

The whole family enjoyed the thrills of the rides at Universal Studios over the next few days, especially the soaking from water rides such as Jurassic Park, but one area they particularly wanted to experience was Harry Potter, which was one of the park's most popular attractions.

Understandably, it was extremely busy and the queues could result in a very lengthy wait. To make it worse, there was no express route, even with the Hard Rock Hotel's room key, so the family had to find another way to avoid standing in the blistering heat for hours.

Although the theme park normally opened at nine o'clock, the gates were open at eight for theme park hotel residents, and on the day they had chosen, the family woke early and were at the entrance shortly after eight. Even at this time, there were still many people heading towards Hogwarts, although the fifteen-minute wait was a considerable improvement on the usual three hours.

At last, the queue of people snaked its way through the rooms of the famous school of magic. Recordings of voices from the film's many characters told their individual stories, every successive room adding to the overall impression so cleverly created by J.K. Rowling in the seven books about the boy wizard.

Inevitably, this being Universal, there had to be a ride within Hogwarts. There were people advising visitors to hurry along on the moving walkways leading up to the ride. Every person had an individual seat with its own hood and seat clamp. Once the ride began to move, the seats tilted in all directions, while a screen in front of each person gave the illusion of being chased by screaming, fire-belching dragons. It was very effective, and everyone agreed it was a superb experience.

The streets and shops described in the Harry Potter stories had also been recreated, and the Kennedy family enjoyed browsing through the shelves of wands, broomsticks and horrible-tasting sweets. These shops were so popular that the organisers permitted a certain number of visitors inside at any one time, closing the doors when it was apparent the confined spaces were too full.

When it came to the Duelling Dragons, Paul and Jason decided to try the extreme ride, while Rebecca and Suzanne preferred to watch.

It was, without doubt, one of the best days of their holiday at Universal Studios and one they felt they would remember for many years to come.

Chapter Two:
An Unwelcome Travelling Companion

ALEX WAS REALLY looking forward to his holiday in Orlando. It was his second visit to the world-famous theme parks, having been there just four years earlier. Now fourteen, Alex felt very grown-up, as his mum and dad had let him travel on his own for the first time, happy in the knowledge that his aunt and uncle, who lived in Orlando, would be meeting him at the airport, from where they would drive to the Universal Theme Park in Florida. The plan was for them to stay at one of the hotels for six days, after which they would drive to his aunt and uncle's home, where he would stay for another week before returning to Orlando airport, ready to fly home.

Alex didn't mind the nine-hour flight from Manchester, landing in Orlando at ten o'clock at night. He filled the time by reading gaming magazines and listening to music on his iPhone. The cabin crew kept a check on him as an assisted passenger. He was quite happy in his own little world, seated in the aisle seat, with two seats between him and the window on the left side of the aircraft. These seats were occupied by a woman with her daughter, Cassandra, who, Alex guessed, was about twelve years old.

Her mother, sitting next to Alex, kept trying to hold a conversation with him, and he feigned sleep to avoid answering. By the time dinner was served, he had actually fallen asleep, and Cassandra's mother shook him gently awake. He mumbled his thanks, grateful he hadn't missed out on the chicken breast with vegetables, followed by chocolate pudding with a rich cherry taste.

Meanwhile, Cassandra complained to her mother about every item on the menu. She was good-looking, although not 'beautiful' in the way most people used the word, but Alex found her distinctly annoying and decided she was spoilt, the way she fussed and complained about the food being unpalatable.

He wasn't particularly interested in girls, preferring instead to spend his time at home, gaming on his PS5, Xbox or computer. He particularly enjoyed multi-player games, where friends and opponents were all online, creating a less-predictable result. To his mind, he was being sociable, talking to others while online, but, when it came to meeting people in the real world, his shyness became apparent, which was why he'd hoped to avoid talking to Cassandra's mother, who unfortunately had other ideas.

"Are your parents going to join you later in Florida?" she asked once their dinner trays had been cleared away.

"No. My dad's a barrister and is in the middle of a big case, so there's no chance of him and Mum going away at the moment. My aunt and uncle live in Florida and are meeting me at Orlando airport."

"Oh, I see." She seemed satisfied with his explanation and picked up the book she'd been reading earlier in the flight—*Inferno*, by Dan Brown, Alex had noticed, as he'd seen and enjoyed the film and thought he would like to read the book one day. Books were usually superior to film versions, but he found reading too slow, when a film could be enjoyed in little over a couple of hours.

Perhaps Cassandra shared his thoughts on books on movies, as while her mother read, she was thoroughly engaged in the in-flight showing on the screen attached to the seat in front of her. As far as Alex could tell, it was one of the many American musicals aimed at teenage girls, a type of film he found quite boring.

The cabin crew came to check on Alex again, talking to him like he was a child, and he answered politely that he was fine. He couldn't wait for the flight to be over. Once he was with his aunt Susie and uncle Andy, he would be treated more like an adult. He smiled to himself remembering how, on his previous visit, Andy had let him drive an electric golf buggy around the quiet roads in the area where they lived, something which would not be possible for a ten-year-old in England. Andy had sat next to him as he drove around the lake, instructing him on which way to steer. At one point, he'd had to make a three-point turn, which he'd felt was quite an achievement.

Until Andy's near-death experience six years earlier, he and Susie had lived near Alex and his mum and dad. Luckily, Andy had the resources from his successful software company to retire to a far more relaxed lifestyle in Florida. They lived near a lake with plenty of wildlife, which brought new interests including hunting. Andy had even let Alex use his gun, shooting at empty drink containers in their large 'backyard'. Alex hoped he'd get to do that again, confident his aim would be much better than it had been four years earlier. The recoil from the gun had taken him by surprise, but he was certain that he could handle the weapon much better now.

He was more adventurous these days, too. He remembered the many happy hours spent at Universal Studios, riding on those roller coasters he'd managed to stomach and which his mum and dad had let him ride. Now he was older, and without them here to cramp his style, he planned to go on some of the bigger, scarier rides, and as the pilot announced they would soon be landing, Alex glanced around the cabin at the many other young people who, like him, were excited for their adventures in the Sunshine State.

Chapter Three:
A Hard Life in Mexico

THE BLISTERING HOT sun shone relentlessly on the tiny, ramshackle houses on the outskirts of Mexico City. In one of these houses, the familiar creak of the kitchen door opening could be heard clearly from the small living area where the children played silently and their father sat in one of the few chairs the family owned.

"Maria!"

The children looked nervously at each other as their angry father shouted for his wife.

"Maria!" he repeated. "Maria!" The aggression in his voice increased with each call.

Enrico, an unkempt, unshaven man in his early forties, kept his eyes firmly fixed on the live ball game showing on the old television in the corner of the room. Even when the crowd cheered loudly, his face showed neither excitement nor pleasure, yet his addiction to the game was evident.

At last, Maria, an anxious-looking woman in her mid-thirties, appeared in the doorway, clutching a bottle of beer.

Raffaele, the eldest of the children, gave his mother a reassuring smile. Timidly, she walked over to her husband, who roughly grabbed the bottle without a word of thanks.

"Where are the rest?" he demanded, his tone uncompromising and harsh.

"I only had enough money for one bottle."

"Liar! I gave you enough for at least three bottles."

Maria coughed nervously. "I needed to buy medicine for Isabella. She has a bad fever."

Enrico turned his bloodshot eyes on Isabella, the youngest of his children, curled up in a rough blanket on the floor. Although it was unbearably hot, the tiny, under-nourished two-year-old was shivering uncontrollably. "She looks all right to me. You spoil the girl."

Maria walked over to her daughter. "She's sick, Enrico! Why can't you see that?" She picked up the child and held her close in a loving embrace, trying to soothe the feverish infant.

"The child will be okay," he growled. "You worry too much."

Somehow, Maria summed up enough courage to take her daughter closer to her husband, hoping he would realise how ill Isabella was. "Look, Enrico! She is sick. If you can't see that, you must be blind!" She regretted the words as soon as they tumbled out of her mouth, but the damage was already done.

The other children shuffled closer together, terrified and surprised their mother was standing up to her bullying husband in a way they had never seen before.

Enrico snapped the top off the beer, took a greedy gulp and slammed the bottle down. Without warning, he grabbed Maria's long hair and pulled hard, bringing her head close to his. She screamed in pain but clung tightly to her crying daughter.

"Don't you ever talk to me like that again, bitch!" His mouth was so close to Maria's face she felt sickened by the smell of his foul breath.

Bravely, Raffaele ran to stand beside his mother. "Leave Mama alone, Papa!"

Enrico released his hold on Maria's hair, turned to face the fourteen-year-old and laughed mockingly. "And just what do you intend to do, you little runt?"

"I…" Raffaele's initial courage was instantly snuffed out by his father's blatant aggression.

Before he had chance to think of a suitable answer, Enrico glared angrily at him and yelled, "Get out! Get out of here! Take the others with you, and don't come back until I tell you to!"

His resolve broken, Raffaele, his sister and two brothers walked meekly out of the room and shut the door behind them. Knowing what would happen next, they each covered their ears, yet it could not block the shouts from their father as Enrico beat his wife yet again. None of them could understand why their father was so horrible and cruel to the woman he had married.

It seemed to take an eternity, but eventually, their mother joined them in the kitchen. Her lip was bleeding, and fresh bruises had appeared on her tired face. No words needed to be spoken as she, holding Isabella in one arm, used the other to comfort each of her children in turn.

Chapter Four:
Teenage Tantrums

THE WIND BLEW hard against Jason's face as he hurtled along the track of the Incredible Hulk. He was thankful for the safety fastenings and body clamp as the carriage turned upside down while still twisting and turning. An unusual feature of the ride was the noise it made: the makers had created a distinctive, howling roar as the carriages sped along, and it could be heard over quite a large area of the park.

Jason glanced sideways at his dad, who seemed to be enjoying the ride and, as always, appeared quite calm. Many girls behind them were screaming loudly, yet these same people would, on the completion of the ride, run to the end of the queue, ready to endure the journey again.

At last, the carriage screeched to a halt, and the body clamps rose automatically. Jason and Paul climbed out, following the crowds of people from the ride. Several were unsteady on their feet after their stomach-churning experience, but even so, they all agreed it was one of the very best rides in the world.

The two walked quickly to the photo collection point where they met Jason's sister Rebecca and her ever-patient mum, who had refused to endure the so-called thrills of the Incredible Hulk. They had already spotted the photographs of Jason and Paul and were laughing loudly at Jason's expression of terror. His mum insisted on buying a photograph, which he knew would be used to embarrass him in the future. Still, he was proud that he had survived the Incredible Hulk.

"Do you think you could manage some food?" she asked, thinking it may not be tempting after such an experience and was surprised by Jason's reaction.

"Oh, yes, please! I'm starving."

They all laughed at Jason's insatiable appetite and set off for one of the many food areas, where Suzanne refilled their large Coke container and bought burgers for all the family.

The sky grew ominously darker as they ate. Within minutes, torrential rain splashed noisily on the hard ground, and everybody quickly sought shelter. Having spent four days at the theme park, the family was used to the extremes of weather and carried ponchos with them at all times, but after ten minutes the downpour eased off, and Paul suggested they took the chance to return to their hotel, since they had exhausted most of the attractions and it was now eight-thirty in the evening.

"Oh, Dad, can't we stay a bit longer?" Jason pleaded.

"No, I think we've done enough for today. We can come back again tomorrow."

"But it's only a bit of rain." It was pointless arguing. His dad wouldn't change his mind.

Rebecca was happy to end their day back at their hotel, but Jason had a long face as they waited for the water-taxi. Many of the passengers were soaked, though the atmosphere was, generally, quite relaxed.

When they reached their suite on the seventh floor of the Hard Rock Hotel, Jason threw himself on his bed in frustration and anger at having to end his fun prematurely. Rebecca came into their room, and he threw his shoe at her. She ducked and it hit the door.

"Don't take it out on me! What's wrong with you?" She often had to bear the brunt of his temper.

"I don't see why we had to come back to the hotel so early. There's nothing to do here!"

"You can always watch the Disney channel," Rebecca suggested. She already knew what his answer was likely to be.

"That's for little kids. There's nothing for teenagers."

Rebecca ignored him, her attention on the view out of their room's window. Torrential rain was splashing hard on the ground, while a vicious storm flashed and clattered noisily overhead. The hotel's huge swimming pool was, understandably, deserted. "Well, I'm happy to be in my room. Just look what it's doing outside."

"I don't care! It's only a bit of rain. We could have gone inside somewhere else. Anywhere would be better than here!"

Giving up on her annoying brother, Rebecca left him and returned to the more relaxed atmosphere of her parents' room. Her mum was writing postcards, while her dad was reading a newspaper, both of them sitting in the comfortable seats close to the large window.

"Jason's in a bad mood," she complained as she picked up her magazine and flopped down on her parents' bed to read. They didn't pass comment. The family was used to the teenager's volatile temperament.

Her dad chuckled at whatever he was reading. "There are some crackpots in this world. This guy…"

Rebecca tuned out while her dad described the article, in great detail, to her mum, who nodded in agreement as she continued to write a postcard.

***

Jason stood at the window, watching the spectacular effects of the storm, which seemed more violent than those they had back at home. "I hate adults! Who needs them? I wish they'd all just disappear and leave us alone. We can look after ourselves." In that instant, a crash of thunder shook the whole building, while flashes of lightning illuminated the room. Mesmerised, Jason stared at the night sky.

***

In the room next door, Rebecca returned from a trip to the bathroom, singing to herself. She settled back on the bed and continued reading her magazine. It was only when she turned to ask her mum a question that she noticed. Her mum and dad were nowhere to be seen. Her dad's newspaper lay on his chair, and her mum's pen and postcards were spread across the table. There were some clothes on the chairs too, which Rebecca assumed were waiting to be put into the suitcases, as they had already been worn. Puzzled, she opened the door to the other room.

"Have you seen Mum and Dad?" she asked her brother.

"No," Jason snapped. "Why would I? I've been in here all the time."

"They've gone."

"Don't be stupid!"

"I went to the bathroom, and when I came back, they weren't there!"

"They can't be far away." Jason followed Rebecca back into their parents' room.

"See!" Rebecca checked the bathroom in case they'd gone in there after her and she hadn't noticed, only to find it empty. Jason opened the outer door and looked up and down the corridor. There was no sign of their parents, and the only sound, apart from the background music and now-decreasing storm, was that of a baby crying.

"Where could they have gone?" Rebecca asked frantically. "They wouldn't just get up and leave without saying a word!"

Jason said nothing and, unusually for him, seemed rather sheepish. The two of them sat quietly on the bed for a while, but Rebecca's impatience, mixed with anxiety, became too much to bear. Huge tears trickled down her face. "I want Mummy and Daddy, Jason. Please find them."

Touched by his sister's anxious state, he put his arm around her shoulder. "I don't know where they are, but I'm certain they won't be long."

Rebecca couldn't remember her brother trying to make her feel better, and it made her suspicious. "Are you *sure* you don't know where they are?"

"I've no idea!" His face flushed red.

"You're lying! I know when you're not telling the truth. Please tell me where they've gone!"

Jason's lips quivered, and his mouth was suddenly dry. "It can't be true... I didn't mean..."

Rebecca's eyes grew wide. Her brother knew something and was concealing it from her. "Just tell me! What have you done?"

"I was angry at having to come back early. It was only a wish. I don't see how..."

"D-did you kill them?"

"No!" Jason was horrified that she'd think that. "I just wished..."

"What, Jason? What did you wish?"

"I...I wished that all adults would disappear, but it can't have come true...can it?"

Rebecca was stunned. "What if it has? Does that mean there are no grown-ups left on Earth?"

"It was only a stupid wish. I don't have that sort of power..." His words trailed off as something else occurred to him. He swallowed and continued. "The storm's stopped now, but when I wished, there was a lot of lightning, and...I'm not certain, but it seemed to be centred around Hogwarts. Perhaps—"

"Switch the TV on!" Rebecca said. Jason compliantly grabbed the remote and jabbed at the controls. "Try CNN."

The children breathed a sigh of relief when they tuned into a CNN financial report, with some deep-voiced city expert being questioned about the state of the US economy.

"There, see! I told you it wouldn't be true!" Jason said, relieved.

"Okay, but that doesn't explain where Mum and Dad are, does it?" As Rebecca spoke, there was a knock on the door, and she ran to answer it, opening it wide. "Mum! D—"

A small boy, about five years old, was standing in the doorway, his eyes red and wet. "Have you seen my mummy and daddy? I can't find them anywhere."

Rebecca didn't know what to say to the distressed child. "Sorry, no. Our parents have also disappeared."

"My baby sister won't stop crying. Can you help me?"

Though she was only a child herself, Rebecca couldn't ignore his plea. "Show me where your sister is."

She followed the boy into the room opposite theirs, while Jason stayed behind. She could hear the cries even before the door was opened fully. A baby, probably only about six months old, lay in a carrycot, screaming for attention. Rebecca hesitated and then picked up the baby. Once in her caring arms, the baby's cries grew less and she seemed more settled.

"What's her name?" Rebecca asked.

"Kelly. What's wrong with her?"

"She just needed attention." Rebecca pulled at the waistband of Kelly's nappy. "And she needs changing."

The boy reared in alarm. "I can't do it!"

Rebecca felt a heavy responsibility settling on her. "If you can find her clean nappies, I'll help you, but I think you should both come into our room for now."

The boy looked devastated. "I want my mummy," he wailed.

"I know you do, but you need to be big and think about Kelly. She needs you to be strong for her. Come on, bring some things, and I'll look after you until your mummy and daddy come back."

In those few, short minutes, Rebecca had grown up into someone who was willing to put her own concerns aside to care for her new, younger friends. Holding Kelly snugly in her arms, she carried her across the corridor to their room, where Jason was still staring at the television and flicking between channels. "Damn!"

"What is it?" Rebecca asked.

"They're all showing recordings! I can't find anything live."

"Oh, no!" The impact of Jason's words hit home immediately. "Does that mean there are no adults *anywhere*?"

"I think so," he answered gloomily.

Chapter Five:
A Disappearing Act

THE AIRBUS WAS flying at fifty thousand feet and was shortly to enter Florida airspace. Three hundred and fifty passengers were looking forward to touching down at Orlando airport, ready for their holiday in the Sunshine State.

"I'm sorry for the extreme turbulence we are experiencing. We should be through this shortly and preparing to land." The captain's calm voice over the plane's speakers did nothing to lessen the effect of the storm as the aircraft lurched and dropped again. The 'fasten seat belts' signs were illuminated and nobody was allowed to visit the toilets, resulting in many complaints from the passengers who did not seem to appreciate the dangers of walking along the aisles in such circumstances.

Even the cabin crew were instructed to remain at their stations until the turbulence had eased.

Alex attempted to read his magazines, undaunted by the rocky ride but unable to ignore Cassandra, who heaved relentlessly into a sick bag despite her mother's stream of comforting words.

The aircraft seemed to become steadier as the captain brought it to a lower altitude and instructed, "Cabin crew, prepare for landing."

Thankful they were able to return to their duties, the crew resumed their walks along the aisles, collecting cups and ensuring that all seats were in the upright position and passengers' seat belts were secure.

"We will be landing at Orlando airport in approximately fifteen minutes, and I would ask that all passengers remain in their seats until…"

Alex peered up at the speaker over his seat, wondering why the captain's message had cut off mid-sentence. He didn't get any further with that thought, however, as there was a commotion along the aisle. Leaning sideways and straining to see past others doing the same, he saw trays, plastic drinking cups and their contents spread over the floor amid mounds of what looked like cabin crew uniforms.

From all over the cabin came cries of dismay as frightened children noticed that every adult in the plane had vanished. Seat belts hung loose as the mass of passengers instantly reduced to about eighty youngsters. Younger children, including several babies, were screaming in panic, while some of the older ones had unfastened their belts and were rushing along the aisles, looking for signs of any adults.

For the first time in the flight, Alex felt a tinge of fear. Cassandra's mother had also disappeared, and the young girl looked horrified. The only sign that her mother had even been there was the book and a pile of clothes on the seat.

The tearful girl looked at Alex. "Don't just sit there looking stupid! Where's my mummy?"

Alex shrugged. "How should I know?"

"Did she go to the toilet?"

"No, she didn't pass me. Besides, her seat belt is still fastened, and her clothes are on the seat."

"But she can't just disappear into thin air!"

"She's not the only one. Look." Alex gestured around him as the two unfastened their seat belts and stood up. "There are only children left." A terrible thought crossed his mind. "If there are no adults, then who's flying the plane?" He started running towards the front of the craft.

"Wait for me!" Cassandra took off after him. Alex was the only person she had known during the flight, and she was determined to stay close to him, even though he was not particularly friendly.

"Get out of the way!" Alex shouted at a group of boys who were blocking the aisle, making it difficult for them to pass.

"What's the rush?" The boys, aged eight or nine, seemed oblivious to the dangers of the situation.

"There's probably no-one flying this plane, since all adults seemed to have vanished! We'll all die unless we do something!"

They immediately parted, letting Alex and Cassandra through.

The situation in the first-class section was identical, with a few children nervously looking around. As the teenagers reached the front of the plane, the door to the flight deck was wide open, which surprised Alex. "I'm sure this door is meant to be locked to prevent terrorist attacks."

"Perhaps one of the cabin crew was leaving the flight deck when they disappeared," Cassandra suggested. "Look." A uniform lay crumpled in the doorway.

"You're probably right."

The two ventured through the open door. As expected, there was no sign of any cabin crew, and the uniforms of the flight captain and navigator lay untidily on the seats. It was eerie to see the empty flight deck with nobody in control. The radio crackled, but there were no voices communicating.

"Shit! We really are on our own!"

Alex removed the clothes and picked up the headset resting on the captain's seat and placed it on his head.

"Hello! Can anybody hear me?"

No reply. Only a low crackle and a great deal of static could be heard. The mass of complicated instruments and controls proved too much for Alex to comprehend. He had flown simulators on his PlayStation, but in the real world, he doubted they'd be much assistance. Glancing around the instruments, he spotted the altimeter. It indicated that they were at three thousand feet and dropping.

"It must be on autopilot, but I don't know if it can land without human control."

"So what can we do?" Cassandra asked, hoping that there was a solution to their awful predicament.

"I really don't know!" Alex answered honestly. "If only there was somebody in the control tower who could tell me how to land, like they do in films. It looks as though the adults have disappeared completely—even those on the ground."

Cassandra shook with fear. In an instant, her whole life had changed, and without adult help, she could soon be dead.

Many thoughts raced through Alex's mind as he desperately tried to think of a solution. The altimeter now indicated 2,500 feet, suggesting a steady descent. He spotted the gauge indicating air speed was at 250 knots: from the sound of the engines, the speed seemed to be dropping, confirmed by the reading. Frustrated by the complexity of the controls, he ripped off the headset and threw it down.

"Perhaps the best thing to do is get out before we crash."

"Without a parachute? Are you mad?"

"We really don't have much choice, do we? It's either jump or burn to death!"

"We're going to die either way!"

"Not if we jump at the right time. Listen, if you want to survive, then help me. Just keep an eye on this meter and shout the readings out every time it changes, Okay?"

Meekly, Cassandra nodded.

"And when the reading reaches a thousand feet, run into the cabin and find me. I'll be near an emergency exit."

Alex's survival instinct kicked in as he rushed out of the flight deck, back into the main cabin area, soon realising that with the noise inside the aircraft, he would have difficulty hearing Cassandra's voice. He spotted a boy of similar age to himself. The teenager, who was well-built with a shock of ginger hair, appeared to be deep in thought.

"Hey, come here!"

The boy looked surprised. "Me?"

"Yes. Quickly!" As he approached, Alex said in as firm and calm a voice as he could muster, "The pilot's gone, and we're going to crash, but there's a chance we'll survive. You can help by listening to Cassandra, the girl in the flight deck, shouting our altitude. When you hear what she says, repeat it, as loud as you can, so that I can hear you. Understand?"

The boy nodded.

"Good!" Alex looked for the emergency exits, trying to find one that was well clear of the wings, since with all the fuel stored within them, they would explode like a bomb on impact.

Once he'd decided which was the safest exit, he scanned the directions printed near the door.

"One thousand seven hundred feet," the boy shouted.

Alex's flight simulator games had taught him that if they opened a cabin door above a thousand feet, the difference in air pressure would result in everything loose being sucked out of the craft.

"One thousand, five hundred feet."

"Listen, everybody!" Alex shouted to be heard. Heads turned towards him. "This plane is going to crash in a few minutes. If you want to survive, come over here!"

Some ignored him yet most came close.

"What's your plan?" one boy asked. "Can you fly this plane?"

"No, I wish I could. Our only chance is to jump when the time is right." Most of the children looked horrified at the thought of jumping out of the plane. "If you stay here, you will definitely die!"

"One thousand, two hundred feet."

The time for action was drawing near, and Alex was as anxious as the others about their chances of survival, but he couldn't show it.

"One thousand feet."

Cassandra ran out of the flight deck towards Alex and a growing group of children. The boy who had been repeating the altitude followed her. With grim determination, Alex began to turn the handle on the inside of the emergency exit. The force of the wind nearly blew him off his feet and whipped the door wide open, displaying what, under any other circumstance, would be a picturesque scene. Between strips of cloud, many coloured lights sparkled in the darkness below them.

Clinging to the closest seat, Alex yelled over the howling wind, "I'll tell you when to jump. As soon as you're out of the plane, grab your legs and try to stay in a tight ball shape—you stand a better chance of survival in that position." He'd taken that straight from his game where commandos had to jump without parachutes and could only hope the technique worked in the real world.

The children around him still looked uncertain, but in a few minutes, the aircraft would smash violently into the ground, and none of them would survive.

The boy who had been shouting the altitudes stepped forward. "I'll go first."

Alex breathed a sigh of relief that somebody was willing to take a chance and, hopefully, encourage the others to follow.

"Thanks. What's your name?"

"Charles. Charles Bradbury."

Alex could see the fear in his eyes and knew how much courage the boy had shown to volunteer. "Right, thanks, Charles." He looked again through the open exit and guessed they were only a few hundred feet above ground. "Okay, Charles. Stand near to the edge and, when you're ready, jump. Good luck!"

Charles stood as close to the opening as he dared and looked down. His legs shook with fear, but he knew that the longer he stayed there, the more difficult it would be for the other children to survive. Gathering the last of his courage, he jumped, letting out a scream as he hurtled downwards.

Alex made a silent wish for Charles and beckoned to the others. Some would die from their injuries, no doubt, but he still believed it was worth the risk. "Come on now. We don't have much time left."

A few children moved towards the door and each, in turn, followed Charles in swift descent. Others were riveted to the spot and it was painfully obvious they could not jump. Alex felt responsible for all these children who were doomed to die, but there was nothing he could do to save them. He just hoped their end would be swift.

Alex noticed that Cassandra had a baby in her arms.

"I can't leave a defenceless baby to die. I'll hold her when I jump."

His impression of her had changed dramatically over the past few minutes. She had transformed from a spoilt child into a thoughtful, caring teenager. "Thanks, Cassy. That's a great idea." He looked around the few children left and picked up a boy of around three years old and moved to the doorway, the infant struggling in his grip.

"Come on. Let's jump together."

With a feeble smile, Cassandra moved to the side of the boy she had known for just a few hours.

Alex could see the outline of buildings indicating they couldn't wait any longer.

The two jumped at the same instant. The wind rushed past their bodies as they hurtled downwards, still clutching the infants. Some of the remaining children followed them, but there were others too fearful to leave the aircraft. Alex was falling fast, too fast to see what was below them; even if it had been daytime, he'd have had no control over where he came down. Clinging tightly to the toddler, who was screaming noisily, he braced for a bone-crushing impact.

Then it happened. The force of the water knocked the breath out of him, and he nearly lost his grasp on the child. As he plunged under the surface, he hit something hard, the impact sending him hurtling upwards again. Grasping the infant's clothing, he tried to swim, searching for signs of land and soon found it. He had fallen into a domestic swimming pool.

What fantastic luck! he thought as he clambered, hoisting the child with him, onto the pool edge. He barely got to his feet when he threw himself to the ground as a terrific explosion rocked the earth and a huge ball of fire lit the night sky. *The plane.*

For a moment, he could only lie there in shock, aware of how much his body ached from the fall, but it didn't feel as if anything was broken. The small boy clung to Alex's arm, sobbing.

"It's okay," Alex said, checking him for injuries. Aside from the shock, he appeared to be all right too. The relief was short-lived, however, as Alex's brain caught up with the past few terrifying minutes.

"Cassy!" He had to find her. Was she still alive? "Cassy!" He called her name several times but without any response.

By now, people should have been coming out of their homes, disturbed by the crash, except there were no people, just the quiet cry of a baby somewhere nearby.

Alex picked up the little boy and followed the sound, traipsing through the gardens of several houses until, at last, he saw the baby lying on the grass and screaming loudly. A few feet away lay the crumpled body of Cassy. Fearing the worst, he turned her onto her back.

"Cassy?"

The streetlights illuminated her face, revealing several long scratches. Her eyes were closed, giving Alex slight hope that she may still be alive.

"Cassy!" She still lay motionless.

Alex had an idea. He set down the toddler. "Hey, buddy, what's your name?"

"Danny."

"Okay, Danny. I'm Alex. Stay there while I help my friend. Can you do that?"

"Hungry."

"I know. We'll see what we can do about that in a bit."

Gathering his long hair in his hands, Alex squeezed it over Cassy's face, dripping cold pool water onto her skin. The girl's eyes flickered open. "Cassy! Thank God! Are you okay?"

As she moved, she flinched in pain. "My back hurts," she said weakly. "All I remember was hitting the branches of a tree—the baby! Where's the baby?!"

Alex picked up the still-crying baby and brought her to Cassy, who was trying to sit up. "Oh, my back!"

"Take it easy. That was one hell of a fall, but the baby seems all right." He handed the small child to Cassy, who was, by now, sitting upright.

She cuddled the baby, shushing her and kissing her head. It was then that she noticed Alex was dripping wet. "What happened to you?"

Alex laughed. "I got lucky and landed in someone's swimming pool, so apart from being soaked, I'm fine."

Seeing huge flames rising in the distance, Cassy thought she knew the answer but still asked, "Is that our plane?"

"Afraid so. Even if the autopilot was enough for it to land, there would be nobody to move aircraft already on the ground out of the way." Alex shuddered at the thought. "I hope those children managed to escape."

Tears welled in Cassy's eyes. "If it wasn't for you, we would all be dead, by now. Thank you so much, Alex."

Embarrassed, he mumbled, "It's okay. We had to do something as long as there was a chance. Now, let's see if you can stand. Here, I'll hold the baby while you try." He took the child and offered his free arm to Cassy. She flinched with every movement, but gradually, she managed to stand upright

"Good! Can you walk?"

She moved forward, a little unsteadily. "I think so."

Alex looked around. "I think we should try these houses and find somewhere to rest for the night. We can figure out the rest tomorrow."

Cassy took back the baby, who was no longer crying, and the four of them approached the front door of the nearest house. Alex hammered on the door, which aroused a vicious-sounding dog. The teenagers looked at each other.

"Let's try the house next door. Hopefully, they won't have a dog." When they repeated the process at the next house along, there was only silence. Alex pushed the door, but it wouldn't open. He led the way around the back of the house; it was a great relief when the kitchen door opened to their push.

Lights were on, but as expected, there was no sign of life. Cassy and Alex called out as they checked each room, hoping to find somebody home. After a few minutes searching, Alex said, "I think there were retired people here. The wardrobe in the bedroom held clothes for a man and a woman, but from their style, they must have been quite elderly." A walking stick lying on the floor next to a pile of clothes seemed to confirm this.

"I'm hungry!" Danny said, tugging on Alex's hand.

"Okay, buddy. There must be some food in the kitchen. Let's have a look."

Thankfully, the cupboards and fridge were well-stocked, and for the time being, the little boy was happy to eat chocolate chip cookies from a jar on the counter. Cassy found some milk and used a small plastic cup, holding it to the baby's mouth. It was difficult without a feeding bottle, and there were several spills, but the baby seemed satisfied.

"We should try and sleep," Alex said, "ready for whatever tomorrow may bring."

"Good idea," Cassy said. There were two bedrooms in the house, and they decided the girls should sleep in one and the boys in the other.

Cassy's blouse and jacket had been torn by the tree, and when she removed them, she used the dressing table mirrors to see long, painful scratches on her back.

Alex hung his and the boy's wet clothes to dry and climbed into the bed, telling Danny to go to sleep. In the night's quiet warmth, they both fell quickly into a deep sleep, disturbed only once during the night by Danny wanting to use the toilet. Alex was not used to playing the part of a father, but after everything else that had happened, it was a walk in the park.

Chapter Six:
A Chance to Escape

RAFFAELE AND HIS younger siblings were helping their mother in the kitchen. It was preferable to being in the room with Enrico, their brutal, intolerant father.

Dolores, a sullen eleven-year-old who closely resembled her mother, helped Maria search for pieces of beef which were not already rotten. There seemed to be more bad meat than good, but eventually, they collected enough to make a simple stew.

Raffaele was busy preparing vegetables to include in the pan. Marco, an energetic eight-year-old, was washing dishes in the sink, while five-year-old Rico dried the dishes, ready for their dinner. Isabella, after being dosed with medicine, slept in a small cot not far from her worried mother.

The smell of the stew cooking cheered up the children, since it was rare to have a decent meal with the little money that was available. They were all aware that their situation would not be so precarious if Enrico would forsake his beer and cigarettes for the good of the family or, even better, seek employment, but this was unlikely to happen.

Eventually, the dinner was ready, and although the children were looking forward to eating, Enrico's presence in the kitchen was feared by all.

As Maria finished serving the stew, she signalled to Raffaele to fetch his father.

Plucking up courage, he gingerly opened the door. "Dinner is ready, Papa." He wished he could have sounded more grown up, but his intimidating father had always weakened his resolve.

Leaving the television on, Enrico looked half-asleep as he stumbled into the kitchen and, without saying a word, sat sullenly at the head of the table. All were silent as they began their meal. Enrico chewed on a piece of meat and to everybody's disgust spat it out onto the plate, splashing gravy over the table. "This food is shit!"

Maria grabbed a cloth and dabbed at the spreading stain on the threadbare tablecloth.

"Stop fussing, woman!" Enrico made a grab for his wife's hair, but at that instant, both adults disappeared into thin air.

There was stunned silence as the children stared in amazement at the empty space where their parents had been only a few seconds earlier.

It was Marco who spoke first. "Where have Mama and Papa gone?"

With increasing consternation, they looked at the chair where their father had been sitting a few moments ago. All that remained was a pile of scruffy clothes.

Raffaele blinked as if this might make a difference. "Perhaps God has taken them, to save Mama from Papa's cruelty and violence."

"If that's true, God would have left Mama to look after us," Dolores said. "We could have managed without that cruel beast!"

After the initial shock, the children decided that, since they could do nothing about their parents' disappearance, they might as well continue with their meal. At least they appreciated the food, even though the meat was a little on the 'high' side.

After their meal, Raffaele went into the living room, thinking he had better switch off the television. He stared in amazement at the screen. A few minutes earlier, the players had been moving swiftly around the ground, cheered on loudly by thousands of spectators. Now, there was just a ball and piles of shorts, shirts and boots all over the pitch, yet no players and not a single spectator to be seen. There wasn't even a commentary. The awful truth hit him hard. He switched off the TV and ran into the kitchen.

"It's not just Mama and Papa who disappeared. I think there are no grown-ups left anywhere in the world."

"But, why? Why would God leave us on our own?" Dolores looked despairingly at her brother. "We really need Mama." She began to cry, her shoulders shaking from the shock of her sudden loss.

Unusually, Raffaele gave her a warm hug. "Don't cry, Dolores. We'll manage. I'm certain Papa will not be able to hurt Mama anymore, as he must be in hell by now."

Feeling at a loss, Raffaele took charge and suggested they all go to bed; Dolores, accepting the role of her mother, took responsibility for Isabella.

When his brothers and sisters were settled down, Raffaele went to visit his friend, who lived a few houses away. His worst fears were realised as Jose related how his parents had also suddenly disappeared. To make it even worse, Dino, his twenty-year-old brother had similarly vanished.

With a heavy heart, Raffaele returned home, his role as the head of the household now confirmed. He wrapped a blanket around himself and lay on the floor, near to his brothers and sisters, and tried to sleep. What was to become of them? Would their parents return? If only his mother were there, everything would be all right, but he had an awful feeling that this world without adults was permanent.

He managed only short, fitful spells of sleep, and by six the next morning, he arose, tired and worried. Without disturbing the others, he slipped quietly out of the house. The morning sun was already hot as he weaved his way through the maze of small, ramshackle dwellings in their part of town until, at last, he entered a more affluent area, where he headed for one house in particular. Raffaele's mother had earned a few extra pesos cleaning for an elderly woman in the house on the corner. He reasoned that, if the old woman had gone, the children could take over her house and live in greater comfort.

Doubts began to fill his mind. What would happen if only the poor adults had disappeared, leaving the wealthy ones alive? Then he thought about the ball game and how everybody had disappeared, regardless of their wealth. He went around the back of the house and pushed at the kitchen door. It swung open. Cautiously, he stepped inside and wandered around the building. He expected that, at any minute, the old woman would appear and ask what he was doing there. It was with great relief that he found the house completely empty. Now he knew what to do, he ran back home and woke the others.

"What is it?" Dolores was tired and annoyed at being disturbed.

"Quickly, all of you. Get up and dressed. Pack some clothes into any bags you can find. I've discovered a new home for us."

"Is Mama there?" The look on Marco's face showed he still hoped for the comfort of his mother's arms.

Raffaele hung his head and shook it slowly. "I wish I could say she is there, but no. She's gone."

Dolores held Isabella while the boys carried what few belongings they had, following their brother. When they reached the big house on the corner, Raffaele pointed, saying, "That's where we're going to live. A mansion of our own."

As they entered through the kitchen, Rico said, "It smells of old people."

Dolores' eyes sparkled on seeing the extent and luxury within the house. "We can soon get rid of that, no problem." The four of them ran from room to room, seeing what was there to discover.

"What happens if the old lady comes back?" Marco asked.

Rico gave a cheeky smile. "We'll say we were looking after the house while she was away."

The others laughed at his brave answer.

More seriously, Raffaele said, "I hope there's some food." They wandered into the huge kitchen area and searched for anything to eat. It seemed as though the old woman had quite a sweet tooth, as they found masses of sweets, chocolate bars, cookies, fresh fruit and fresh juice. Not used to such luxuries, they all over-indulged, particularly on the chocolate bars.

Marco, with mouth nearly full and chocolate smudged on his lips had a sudden thought. "Does this mean we don't need to go to school anymore?"

Raffaele laughed. "Well, you can still go there if you want, but there won't be any teachers to shout at you for getting things wrong!"

They all clapped their hands in excitement. Just twenty-four hours earlier, they would have been in serious trouble with Enrico for making such noise, but now they felt the exhilaration of freedom from their tyrannical father.

After eating their fill, the children had a look at the bedrooms. Although the old woman lived on her own, there was a second bedroom and, best of all, there were actually beds. Real beds! After years of sleeping in rough blankets on the floor, this was pure luxury.

When the children walked into the en-suite bathroom, their eyes grew wide in amazement at the sight before them. Never had they seen a proper bath or a flushing toilet, and without shyness, they all queued patiently to use the convenience.

When they had all exhausted their bladders and curiosity, Raffaele spoke quietly to Dolores. "I'm going back to the house to get a few more of our things. Will you look after them, please?"

"Yes, of course, but don't be long."

Raffaele left and made his way back to the shack that had been his home for the past fifteen years. It seemed strange as he gathered what he could of their meagre belongings into a couple of plastic bags and hurried to leave. He would not miss this place of so many bad memories.

As he left, his friend, whom he had spoken to the previous evening, saw him. "Raffaele! I called and found nobody at home."

"We moved out to a proper house in the suburbs. Why did you want me, Jose?"

"I've been talking to a few of my friends about what we should do, now there are no adults to order us around. Pepe's father used to drive the school bus, and Pepe, having learned from his father, feels he could drive us anywhere we want to go."

Raffaele was puzzled. "Why would you want to go away from the area?"

"Because we can!" was Jose's simple answer. "Just think of it—we can go anywhere, and there is nobody to stop us. No police!"

"But where would we go? We know where we are if we stay here."

"True. But what would you say if I told you we were thinking of going to Universal Studios and Disney in Florida?"

Raffaele's jaw dropped at the thought of going to the place most poor Mexican children could only dream of. "How?"

"Think about it, Raffaele. There's no president, no police or border patrols, so no problems getting into North America anymore and no drug cartels killing anyone who gets in their way." A huge smile lit Jose's face at the thought of freedom of movement throughout the whole country. "We don't need money, as we can take what we want, and the bus can fit about forty children."

"It sounds good," Raffaele admitted. "When?"

"Tomorrow morning. Pepe is busy filling the bus and making certain it's ready for such a long run."

"Let me speak to the others first. If they agree, then we will be here tomorrow morning."

As Raffaele returned to their new home, he had mixed feelings. The idea excited him, yet it would mean moving out of their newfound luxurious accommodation.

Dolores noticed the troubled look on her brother's face. "What's wrong?"

He quickly explained his dilemma.

The idea appealed to Dolores, yet she said, "We need to ask Marco and Rico. If we do it, we do it as a family."

He agreed, and without delay, they explained the idea to the younger boys.

"Will I get to meet Mickey Mouse and Minnie Mouse and all the others?" Rico asked, excited at the prospect of meeting these famous magical characters.

"I hope so," Raffaele lied. The Disney characters were ordinary people in costumes, so it was unlikely he'd be able to keep his promise.

Marco was equally keen to see the magic of Disney, and although they now had a comfortable lifestyle in their new house, the attractions of Florida were too strong to resist.

For the rest of that day, the four children enjoyed the foods they could find, while Dolores made sure Isabella had enough nourishment.

That night, for the first time in their lives, all five children slept in comfortable beds. It seemed a shame to lose this for an uncertain future many miles away, but the life-changing decision had now been made.

Chapter Seven:
The Awful Truth

JASON AND REBECCA had checked some of the other hotel rooms, finding several frightened children, yet there were still no signs of any adults. Many of the children were between six and ten years old and all asked where their parents could be. By now, Rebecca felt certain that her brother's deathly wish had really come true, and somehow, they had to live with the consequences. She was sensible enough not to reveal this to anyone as she tried to console the terrified children.

Jason's guilt had changed him, and he was genuinely concerned for the mass of orphans they had discovered. Rebecca was still carrying the baby, while Kelly's brother, Peter, stayed close by. It was nearly ten o'clock, and Rebecca, feeling tired, decided she needed sleep and returned to their room.

"Can you bring Kelly's carrycot into our room, please, Jason? I think we all need to get some sleep."

Her brother meekly complied, saying that he would sleep in the bed in his parents' room. After tucking Peter into Jason's bed, Rebecca climbed into the other, leaving the carrycot between the beds. It took a while, but eventually, she fell into a troubled sleep.

When she awoke the next morning, Rebecca wondered if it had all been a bad dream, but when she saw the baby and Peter still asleep, the awful truth came back to her. If only she could hug her mum and dad, everything would be all right, but there would never be another chance for such comfort.

Kelly had woken during the night, but Rebecca had brought her feeding bottle and powdered milk into her room and was, thankfully, able to feed the baby. The responsibility of acting as 'mother' to Kelly and Peter weighed heavily on her, and in those few short hours, she had matured noticeably. She lay there quietly for a while until she heard Peter stirring.

He sat up in bed, looked around and promptly burst into tears. "I want my mummy and daddy!"

"Listen, Peter. I'm also missing my parents, but we don't know where they've gone. All we can do is look after ourselves."

"I'm hungry!" Peter wailed inconsolably. Rebecca offered him a few biscuits, which kept him quiet for the time being. Kelly was still asleep, and Rebecca decided to lie in her bed for a bit longer. She thought about the smiling, helpful catering staff in the restaurant and knew that today, there would be nobody to greet them or prepare breakfast. She just hoped they could find enough food to satisfy their hunger, but for how long? Tears filled the young girl's eyes as she pondered the possibilities of a very uncertain future. With a heavy heart, she climbed out of bed, went to the bathroom and washed her face. She nearly had a shower but then thought, *What's the point?*

Returning to the bedroom, she asked, "Peter, do you have a pushchair for Kelly?"

"Yes, in our room." The boy looked excited. "Are we going to look for Mummy and Daddy?"

She felt bad as she lied, "I think we should go to the restaurant, but we will keep looking for them. Okay?"

The boy seemed happier at the prospect of finding his parents. "Okay."

Rebecca pushed the door open to the adjoining room. "Jason! Wake up!"

Her brother stirred and turned to face her. "What is it? Are Mum and Dad back?"

"What do you think?" Her sarcastic reply reflected the blame she placed on her brother. "They're never coming back, thanks to you! We should go to the restaurant and see what we can find to eat."

"Oh, shit!" He pulled off the untidy covers and jumped out of bed. "I was hoping it was all a bad dream."

"Careful with your language. Remember we're looking after a small boy and his baby sister. Come on, hurry up. I'm hungry."

Jason quickly pulled on his clothes and followed.

They found Kelly's pushchair, placed the baby inside and Rebecca took responsibility for pushing the infant. They could have looked in the Club lounge but instead decided to take the lift down to the ground floor and head for one of the large restaurants.

As they walked, many children seemed to be wandering aimlessly, all in a state of shock and confusion. The sight which met them on entering the restaurant shocked them even more. Many tables bore part-eaten meals, cutlery lying where the adults had dropped it at the point when they had disappeared. Trays with leftover food, broken plates and dishes littered the floor. The grilling hobs were blackened by the overcooked meats left by the missing chefs. Fires had broken out in some cooking areas, but sprinklers had extinguished the flames, leaving a sodden, blackened mess.

Piles of clothes lay abandoned where the adults had either been sitting or standing as their bodies vanished.

Jason eyed scene of devastation in dismay, feeling that he was solely responsible for what was happening. "Let's look in the kitchens to see what we can find to eat."

As they pushed the doors open, a similar scene met them. Part-prepared foods lay on the worktops, while water was pouring from a tap, presumably because somebody had turned it on just before they had disappeared. Jason turned it off and looked around for something salvageable.

The newly responsible Rebecca had a suggestion. "Fruit, bread and cakes are going to be the safest things to eat. See what you can find, Jason." The pushchair came in handy, as it had a zip-up bag attached to it. The two of them found apples, bananas, oranges, many wrapped cakes and biscuits, which they plundered to fill the bag. Rebecca gave some cake to Peter, who hungrily devoured it. There was still plenty of food left, which, no doubt, other children would soon find.

The nagging question remained: What happened when the food ran out?

Chapter Eight:
A New Way of Life

ALEX AWOKE TO an unexpected smell. Initially confused by his strange surroundings, he sat up and sniffed the air. "Bacon!" The salty aroma of bacon cooking was unmistakable. He pulled on his clothes and wandered through to the kitchen, where Cassy was busy preparing breakfast. This was nothing like the spoiled girl he had met on the previous day's flight from Manchester. Eggs were frying while bacon sizzled gently on the grill.

"Can I help?" Alex felt he should do something useful.

"You could find some knives and forks and lay the table. I think you should also wake Danny so he can have breakfast with us."

Obediently, Alex returned to the bedroom. "Danny!"

The boy stirred, his eyes flickered open, and he looked at Alex.

"Where's my mummy and daddy?"

"I don't know, Danny. Cassy and I will look after you for now. Are you hungry?" Alex could see the pain in his young face.

Danny climbed wearily out of the bed and followed Alex silently into the dining area. He looked so sad that the main people in his life had literally vanished.

"Would either of you like some toast?" Cassy had assumed the role of mother, accepting this strangest of situations without question.

"Yes, please," Alex answered. Danny didn't respond to Cassy's question. "He seems traumatised, but I would give him some to build up his reserves." All of them needed to eat while they had food, since they had no idea where their next meal would come from. "How is the baby?"

"All right, I think. She woke me up several times during the night. I mixed a biscuit with milk to feed her, and it worked—for now."

Alex was impressed by Cassy's determination to be responsible for their welfare. "You're doing a great job, Cassy."

The teenage girl blushed at his praise.

"How's your back after your fall into the tree?"

"Oh, it's not bad. A few scratches and a few aches, but that's all."

Cries from the bedroom indicated the baby was awake. Alex went to get her, leaving Cassy to finish preparing breakfast.

As Alex carried the child in, he said, "We don't even know what she is called."

"I've been thinking about that. She looks so angelic, I thought it would be nice to call her Angela. She's young enough to adopt a new name."

Alex took a seat at the table with the now quietened child on his knee. "It sounds as though you've accepted the adults aren't coming back?"

"What else can we assume?" Cassy was about to say something else when she realised that to say anything more would probably upset Danny. Instead, she finished organising breakfast and piled the food on the three plates. "Let's make the most of what we've got, okay?"

"Yes, of course." Alex was hungry and enjoyed the breakfast Cassy had prepared for them. His mind was in turmoil.

Noticing his absent expression, Cassy asked, "What are you thinking?"

"I was wondering what we should do next. We could stay here, but eventually, the food will run out. And then what?"

"There must be some stores where we can find food. At least we don't need to worry about money."

Alex knew this could be only a short-term solution. "At some stage, the food will still run out. Don't forget, there will be thousands of hungry children just like us with the same idea, and any fresh food will rot without being replaced."

"So what should we do, then?"

Alex shrugged in despair. There were limited options open to them. "I wish I knew. Maybe we should try to get to somewhere else."

Once they were finished eating, Alex went into the bedroom and picked up his iPhone. Since it had been in a zipped-up pocket in his jacket, it was damp, but it had survived the fall.

Nervously, he switched it on and tried dialling his home number in England. He was hoping beyond hope that his parents were still alive. With no answer from his mother, he tried his dad's mobile, but again received no response. Even allowing for the time difference, they would have answered if they were able to. A heavy feeling filled his heart as he walked back into the kitchen.

"I tried phoning home. It seems the problem isn't restricted to America. That's over seven and a half billion people affected. I wonder how many children are left."

"I was afraid of that," Cassy said carefully. "Do you have any teenage relatives?"

Alex's heart lifted at this question. "Cassy, you're brilliant!" He returned to the bedroom and scrolled through his contact list and called his cousin Robert, then waited, with rising impatience, as the line rang out.

His heart lifted when the familiar voice answered. "Hi, Alex! I thought you were in the States."

"I am, Rob. Are your mum and dad there?"

"They must still be in bed. I've not seen them, yet. Why?"

Realising his cousin was not yet aware of the disaster, Alex chose his words carefully. "Can you go and see if they're there?"

He could hear Rob running up the stairs. "Why? Is there a problem?"

"Just look first and then I'll explain."

He heard the knock on the bedroom door, followed by a gasp of surprise. "They're not here! Where have they gone? How did you know they wouldn't be here?"

Again, Alex took a deep breath. "You've confirmed my worst fears. While I was flying here last night, all the adults disappeared, and I only managed to avoid death by jumping from the plane. There are no adults where I am. I needed to know if it had affected more than America."

There was stunned silence from Rob and then, finding his voice, he said, "You must be joking!"

"I wish I was. If you don't believe me, look through the window and tell me if you can see any adults."

He heard Rob pulling back the curtains in the bedroom. After a pause, he asked, "You mean there are no adults anywhere in the world?"

"That's exactly what I mean. I wish I could say it was an April fool's joke. Something happened last night, and it looks as though there are only children left here on Earth."

"That must be why I didn't see Mum and Dad last night. I thought they'd gone out without letting me know. What are we going to do?"

"I really don't know, but at least there won't be any schools, as there are no teachers."

Rob laughed. "That is a definite bonus, but there are also no farmers, engineers or anybody who helps to keep the world running."

"True. Listen, Rob. See what you can find out, keep your mobile charged and send me texts when you can. It does mean I'm stuck in Florida, as there's no way of getting back. I have a friend in Singapore, so I'll phone her next and find out if the same happened to her."

"Wish I was stuck in Florida, you lucky devil! Bye, Alex."

Alex scrolled down the list on his mobile and found Jasmine, a fourteen-year-old Indian Singaporean he'd met on holiday two years earlier. When she answered, it was obvious she was pleased to hear from him. She confirmed that all adults in her area had disappeared that morning. It had come as a great shock for Jasmine and her five younger siblings, who were struggling to accept their new, precarious situation. She agreed to keep in touch with Alex by text message and wished him luck.

Alex decided to tell Cassy about his findings later and looked around the house, searching for a bag or anything they could use to carry enough food to last them for a while. Eventually, he found a rucksack pushed into the back of a bedroom cupboard. It looked quite old, as though it had not been used for many years. He tipped it upside down, allowing the contents to spill out onto the floor. Numerous photographs lay in an untidy heap; unable to dismiss his curiosity, he gathered a few together and scanned through them. They were photos of a soldier, back from the Vietnam War in the late sixties. It seemed so sad that someone who had survived such a terrible war had now vanished as though they had never even existed. Alex picked up the rucksack and took some of the photos to show to Cassy. "Hey, look at these."

She found it equally interesting to discover the history of the occupants of the house they had taken over like squatters. She picked out one of the photographs and held it close to a photograph hanging on the wall. It showed a man and woman, probably both in their late eighties, taken on a cruise ship. The man's features, compared with the old photos and allowing for nearly sixty years of aging, were definitely the same.

Cassy studied the picture more closely. "They looked so happy."

"Yes. It's so sad. After all they must have been through over the years, they're no longer here."

"I don't know who's luckier. At least they don't have an uncertain future like us." The look of despair in Cassy's eyes was unmistakable.

Alex put his arm around the girl's shoulders. "Listen, Cassy. Don't give up. We have to do what we can to survive. It's not going to be easy, but we have to try. I'll do everything I can to make certain that we'll be all right. Okay?"

Encouraged by his words, Cassy nodded and took the rucksack into the kitchen. "Okay, let's see what we can find." They began opening cupboards and drawers until every storage space had been checked. Fortunately, the couple who had lived in the house had stocked up quite a bit of food. Cassy handed everything to Alex, who began to fill the bag with goodies. Oranges, apples, bananas, fruit juice and anything else suitable were added: the bag was not yet full but still quite heavy.

"Perhaps we should stay here one more night, Cassy. It's already mid-afternoon, so we may be better waiting until tomorrow."

Cassy agreed and checked what she could cook for an afternoon meal. In a way, she was pleased to wait another day, as her injuries from the fall were still painful.

After a dinner of steak and potato fries, Alex took charge of Danny and Angela, while Cassy enjoyed a relaxing bath. She managed to find cream to apply to her scratched skin, and that evening, she fell into a very sound, restful sleep.

After breakfast the following morning, they collected all their provisions and prepared for a long journey into the unknown.

Mindful of the small baby in their care, Cassy filled a flask with milk, which, with some crushed biscuits, would provide sustenance for a short while.

Alex pulled the bag onto his back and, together with Cassy, Danny and baby Angela, left the house they had borrowed for the past two days.

As they turned onto the road, Alex stopped.

"What's wrong?" Cassy asked.

"I can't decide which way we should walk. I've no idea where we are, so…left or right?"

Cassy understood his dilemma. The choice of direction could affect their future, whatever was left of it. Boldly, she said, "I think left." She pointed along the road. "Before you ask, I don't know why, but let's try it anyway."

Accepting her decision, Alex began walking, holding Danny's hand, while Cassy carried Angela.

They had not walked far before evidence of the catastrophe could be seen. Many cars, which presumably were being driven at speed when the drivers disappeared, had crashed, some more violently than others. Two cars had crashed head-on, leaving a burnt-out, mangled wreck in the middle of the road. It was sad that all these vehicles, once prized possessions of their owners, were now useless heaps of scrap metal.

After walking for about ten minutes, Alex was surprised to hear the sound of a powerful engine disturbing the strangely silent world. He turned to see an open-topped sports car heading towards them. He was even more surprised when the car horn sounded, and the vehicle drew up beside them.

It was Charles, the boy who had volunteered to jump first out of the aircraft. "Hey! I never thought I'd see you guys again."

Alex smiled. "I'm pleased you landed safely."

Charles laughed. "I was lucky. I fell into a lake. Got very wet but, thankfully, nothing broken. Spent a while in a house. Had to break in, but there's nobody to stop us now."

"We also found a house to stay for the last two nights. Where did you get the car?"

"I didn't fancy hanging around here and was lucky to find a car which hadn't been wrecked. The key was in the ignition and it's an automatic. Really easy to drive. Can I give you a lift?"

Alex looked at the small sports car and realised it would be quite a crush for them all to fit. "Thanks, but no. You've given me an idea, though. If we can find a larger car with keys, I should be able to drive it. Do you want to help us find one so we can stay together?"

Charles wasted no time weighing up the suggestion. "Sorry, guys, but I don't fancy being held back by small kids. If you don't mind, I think I'll stay on my own."

"Okay, it's up to you." Alex felt a little disappointed that, after meeting up with Charles again, he didn't want to stay with them.

"Good luck!" Charles waved and sounded his horn as the car accelerated along the road, disappearing from view.

The small group continued walking, Alex now looking at every abandoned vehicle, hoping to find something suitable for them. After walking for about thirty minutes, he spotted an eight-seater Ford. The door was partly open, as though the driver was either getting in or out when they had disappeared. "Yes!" Alex found the key in the ignition and felt triumphant at discovering something suitable.

"Are you sure you can drive this thing?" Cassy asked uncertainly.

"I think so. What have we got to lose?"

"Our lives?" Cassy answered sardonically.

"Listen, we jumped out of a plane and somehow survived it. Driving a car is going to be tame by comparison. Just give me a chance to try to get us somewhere."

"Okay, but please don't drive fast." Cassy slid the passenger door open and lifted Danny inside. She fastened his seat belt and then sat beside him. Without a child's car seat, she had no option but to hold Angela on her lap.

Alex familiarised himself with the controls and instruments. Thankfully, it was an automatic drive.

"I hope it has plenty of petrol or we won't get very far," remarked Cassy.

"Just a minute and I will know." He turned the ignition key. The dials on the dashboard lit up. Another quarter turn and the engine started. Alex looked at the fuel gauge. "The tank's about two-thirds full, which should take us quite a distance."

"Where shall we go?"

Alex smiled at his doubtful companion. "I've been thinking about that. Why don't we look for Universal Studios? After all, that's where we would have gone if the adults hadn't disappeared, leaving us in the lurch. There's bound to be plenty of signs to direct us there."

Cassy had to admit Alex's idea was a good one, and the thought of still going to Universal Studios excited her. "Okay, I'll keep a lookout."

"Right, hold on tight." If Alex was honest, the prospect of driving frightened him, but he thought better of mentioning this. He released the handbrake and pushed the lever in to the drive position. With his foot pressing the accelerator pedal, they began to move forward a bit faster than Alex had anticipated. "Sorry." He eased the pressure off, and they drove along the road at about thirty miles an hour. After a few minutes, he was gaining confidence and skilfully manoeuvred around the many abandoned cars.

"Alex! Stop!" Cassy shouted.

He slammed on the brakes, bringing the car to a sudden halt. "What is it?"

The girl pointed to a crashed car. He followed her gaze and then realised why this car was different from all the hundreds of other crashed vehicles they had already passed. It was Charles in the sports car, the front of which was badly damaged, having hit a fire hydrant, and Charles looked unconscious.

Alex turned off the engine and jumped out. He ran over to the wreck. "Charles!" He threw the door open and dragged the boy out. He hadn't been wearing a seat belt, and Alex was worried about the extent of his injuries. There was heavy bruising to his face, but thankfully, he began to regain consciousness. "What happened?" Alex asked.

"I was trying to avoid a car on the road and skidded," Charles answered groggily. "I think I may have been going a bit too fast."

"I can imagine. Think you might be safer travelling with us, Charles."

"You might be right, Alex." He smiled weakly and then winced.

"Don't worry, it will soon heal," Alex consoled. He slid the door back and helped Charles to climb in behind Cassy before returning to the driving seat. Alex started the engine again, and they pulled away onto the freeway.

"Where are you heading?" Charles asked.

"Universal Studios. You can help by looking out for signs. It can't be too far away."

Charles smiled at the thought. "That sounds like a great idea."

"Is your seat belt fastened?" As a novice driver, Alex thought the chances of an accident were quite high, with or without any other drivers on the road.

Charles obediently fastened his belt. "Yes, sir!"

Alex liked Charles' jovial nature and hoped the group could survive a world without adults.

It was amazing how many cars had crashed. Some had collided head-on, resulting in tangled wrecks, while others had careered off the road, ending up in the middle of a neat, manicured lawn, like strange pieces of industrial artwork.

Suddenly, Alex slammed on the brakes and screeched to a halt. Beside him, Cassy groaned, clinging tightly to the children.

"I can't get through. There are cars all across the road." He unfastened his seat belt and was about to leave the vehicle to check the situation when he spotted something out of the corner of his eye. A group of at least fifteen teenagers, all brandishing baseball bats, emerged from behind bushes.

"Hold on tight," shouted Alex. He jumped back into the driving seat, put his foot down hard on the accelerator and headed towards a small gap between the line of cars. There was a terrific noise of metal grinding on metal as the people carrier charged through the barricade of lighter cars. Some of the threatening teenagers jumped back as they realised Alex did not intend stopping for them. It was a great relief when the people carrier finally crashed its way through and accelerated along the road. Alex could, through his rear-view mirror, see some of the teenagers angrily waving their baseball bats at the fast-disappearing vehicle.

"Phew! That was close. They didn't seem very friendly." This understatement from Charles made them aware of how dangerous the world had become with the demise of adults.

"What do you think they wanted?" asked Cassy.

Alex shrugged. "Who knows? It could have been our transport, the food we brought with us or they were just looking for trouble."

Cassy was shaken at the thought that, even with the disappearance of adults, violence was still a disturbing feature of this modern world.

They'd been driving in silence for about twenty minutes when Alex exclaimed, "I think I know where we are! I recognise those shops over there, which means my uncle's house isn't far from here. Hope you guys don't mind if we stop there?"

Cassy and Charles couldn't understand why Alex wanted to stop, knowing that his relatives wouldn't be there, but they had no objections.

As if reading their minds, he said, "I just want to see their home for the last time." He was gaining confidence in his driving and skilfully avoided all the crashed vehicles as he turned off the main road. A few minutes later, he pulled up into the drive of a smart, single-storey house, typical of many found in Florida. "Do you guys want to come in with me?"

Cassy had already unfastened her seat belt and was helping Danny out of his seat. "Yes, I think we should stick together."

Charles seemed undecided but stiffly followed Alex. The entrance to the house was from a covered carport, but when Alex tried the door, it was firmly locked. Undaunted, he walked around the back and lifted a plant pot from a plastic tray. With a triumphant cry, he picked up the key which had been hidden under the plant. Returning to the kitchen door, he inserted the key and turned it.

Nervously, he pushed the door open wide and entered, followed by the others. Alex half-expected to find his uncle in the reclining chair, sipping a cool beer, watching war documentaries on television in the living area, while Susie would be busy in the kitchen, preparing some delicious, typically American meal, but of course, there were absolutely no signs of life. Alex sighed despondently.

"They were probably visiting friends when they disappeared."

Sensing his anguish, Cassy laid a comforting hand on his arm. As he turned to face her, she saw the sadness in his large, brown eyes. "You were very close to your aunt and uncle, weren't you?"

He nodded. "I hoped that one day, I could come and live here with them. It was one of my life goals to emigrate to America."

Cassy had always loved England and couldn't imagine living anywhere else, but now it seemed her chances of returning home were remote. The closest person in Cassy's life was her mother, as her parents had divorced when she was only three years old. Although her father had access rights, she had seen very little of him over the years.

"Food!" Snapping out of his sad thoughts, Alex decided action was necessary. "My uncle always made sure there was plenty of food in the house, so we might as well stock up."

He walked to a door at the back of the kitchen area and pushed it wide open. The pantry was stacked high with every type of food possible. "My uncle was in the army before he went into business and believed in always having plenty of provisions in stock."

It really was like an Aladdin's cave, with hundreds of tins of beans, soups, meat and puddings as well as countless boxes of cereals and biscuits. Best of all, there were packets of dried fruits, like mango and pineapple, which were highly nutritious. It would be impossible to take everything, but soon Alex and Charles had packed several boxes full of the most useful foods and drinks.

Cassy was looking after Danny and Angela, cradling the baby in her arms. Aware of a sudden noise outside the house, she looked through the front window and screamed.

"What's wrong, Cassy?"

She pointed to the window. "Someone's trying to damage our car. Look! It's rocking!"

As Alex looked through the window, he saw three large figures coming around the near side of the vehicle. "Bears!" he shouted.

The three teenagers watched on in horror as the bears used their enormous strength to try and tip the car over. Alex rushed back to the pantry and returned carrying a shotgun.

Cassy looked alarmed. "What are you going to do?"

"My uncle always had a problem with bears around here and used his shotgun to scare them away. They come hunting for something to eat. Did anyone leave food in the car?" He'd brought the rucksack into the house and wondered why the bears were still attacking the car.

Charles grimaced. "I think I might have left a couple of chocolate bars in the pocket near my seat."

"Was the car door open?" Alex knew the answer before Charles replied.

"Afraid so. I didn't think it mattered." Charles lowered his eyes guiltily.

With a quick check of the supply of pellets for the shotgun, Alex moved to the kitchen door. "Stay here and keep the door shut." Silently stepping out, he crept towards the front of the house. As he turned the corner, he could see the three bears pushing hard against the vehicle. Aiming his shotgun at the backside of the nearest bear, he pulled the trigger. The hungry bear immediately dropped down on all fours and scampered away back to the forest. Before Alex had a chance to aim for the second bear, the car fell on its side with a heart-rending crash of glass and metal. It must have shocked the bears, as they quickly lumbered after the first bear.

Alex looked at the vehicle with an anxious feeling gnawing at the pit of his stomach. This was not supposed to happen. The car had been their only means of escape. Universal Studios was, above all else, the place where he wished to be, but how?

He returned to the kitchen and looked gloomily at the others. "I don't think that car is going to be of any use to us now."

The three of them stood in mournful silence, staring out at the upended vehicle.

"Are you sure your aunt and uncle were somewhere else when it happened?" Cassy asked.

"Why? What are you thinking?"

"Well, they have a carport and a garage, and—"

"The garage!" Alex rushed back into the carport and pushed a door on the far wall. "You're right, Cassy! There's another car in here!" It was a Chevrolet, a five-seater sedan, and smaller than the people carrier, but it was big enough for them. Alex found the keys and turned the ignition: it was just over half full of gas, which should be plenty.

"We should stay here tonight," Cassy said.

Alex liked the idea of staying in his aunt and uncle's house. Just one more night would do no harm. It wasn't as though there were any time limits on them getting to Universal Studios.

Cassy found it easy to make a meal for them on the modern hob, with Charles's assistance, while Alex looked after Danny and Angela.

They relaxed for the rest of that day, watching recorded documentaries on the large television in the living area. A second night in a comfortable bed helped them to regroup for the next day.

Cautiously looking for any wandering bears, Alex and Charles made several journeys between the kitchen and the garage, loading the car with as many boxes as they could fit. Alex returned to the pantry for the shotgun and all the boxes of pellets. He then wandered into the bedroom and slid open a drawer at the side of the bed. Alex knew, from what his uncle had told him, that he kept a loaded revolver there. Not far away was a box of cartridges, which he slipped into his pocket.

Cassy looked scared when she saw what was in Alex's hands. "Do we really need a gun?"

"I…I don't know, but I think it's best we prepare for the worst. You saw that mob of kids at the road block yesterday." He opened the garage doors wide and hurried into the driving seat.

Charles sat next to Alex, while Danny and Cassy, with Angela on her knee, were in the back of the car.

Chapter Nine:
A Search for Life

As Jason, Rebecca and the two young children left the grounds of the Hard Rock Hotel, they didn't bother going to the jetty; they knew the usually jovial captain wouldn't be there. Instead, they took the long path that led around the perimeter of the lake, upon which various abandoned vessels and toys—small boats, dinghies, jet-skis and oversize inflatable rings—bobbed gently.

About halfway to Universal's entrance, they noticed the ferry boat floating about fifty feet offshore. Several young, frightened children on board were shouting for help. Jason and Rebecca watched on helplessly, not sure how to rescue these children. Then Jason had an idea.

"That big inflatable ring we saw! We could use that to get them to safety."

Rebecca wasn't sure what her brother had in mind but was pleased he was willing to help. "I'll stay here and look after the children."

Jason ran back along the path and soon returned with the inflatable ring. It was about five feet in diameter with four handles, the type in which people would usually float lazily. Jason took off his shoes, socks and T-shirt then threw the ring onto the water and jumped in beside it.

The water was cooler than he'd expected and a welcome contrast to the blistering-hot sun.

Jason was a strong swimmer but was thankful the boat wasn't too far from the bank. Once there, he told three of the youngsters to jump into the water. As each jumped, he helped them to hold on to one of the rubber handles. The children were terrified, but with Jason's help, they soon reached the bank. Making sure they were safe, he returned to the boat. Within half an hour, eight grateful children, all aged around four or five years old, stood in puddles on the riverbank, but they would soon dry in the sun. They watched in awe as Jason put his T-shirt, socks and shoes back on. To those eight children, the tall, skinny teenager was a hero.

"You were great!" Rebecca said, giving her brother a hug of gratitude. She knew that his reformed character was a result of his guilt, but she didn't mention it.

Embarrassed, Jason jollied the children along, and they continued their walk towards the theme park. Rebecca pushed Kelly's pushchair, with Peter and the eight children by her side.

It was at that point Peter realised. "Where are all the mummies and daddies?"

"I don't know," Rebecca replied, deciding it was better to leave the child in ignorance than try to explain that her brother had wished them away. By now, the sun was quite strong, but they'd left the sun cream back in their hotel room. Tears filled her eyes as she imagined her mum saying, *"You're not going out in that without sun cream. You don't want to get skin cancer, do you?"*

Rebecca's heart felt heavy as they entered the theme park, her interest considerably diminished. There were stores dotted around, most selling souvenir T-shirts and other memorabilia, but in one store, she spotted sun cream.

"Wait here with the little ones," she instructed Jason and made a beeline for the store, loading several bottles of sun cream into the pushchair's bag.

Returning to the group, she opened one of the bottles and liberally spread it over all the children's skin. Even Jason, realising how important it was both for their safety and for his sister's well-being, let her apply the cream to his face, neck, arms and legs. Finally, Rebecca used it for herself before continuing their tour of the park.

Some of the attractions were no longer operating, as they needed constant adult maintenance and intervention. This caused a great deal of frustration for the children, who would have been quite happy to continue using the rides, especially without their parents around to ruin their fun.

Chapter Ten:
A Long Journey

RAFFAELE WAS USED to the sound of his brothers' snoring, but it disturbed him more, now they were all together in the same bed. He'd thought that the comfort would help him, but it was so different from what he was used to, it made restful sleep impossible. He lay awake, thinking of his newfound situation and wondering what the future held for him and his siblings.

By five a.m., he'd had enough of lying in bed and wandered into the bathroom. He was curious about the over-bath shower and thought he would like to try it out. He took the handset off the wall and, turning the tap, was shocked at the pressure of the jet of water shooting from the head. He quickly turned it off and undressed, dropping his clothes untidily onto the floor. Now naked, he stepped back into the bath and held the shower handset away from him as he turned on the water again.

This is luxury, he thought as the powerful jets hit his skinny body.

Marco and Rico had heard the noise and wandered in to see their brother enjoying the shower.

"Come on in," shouted Raffaele. "It's great!"

It did look fun, and very soon, all three were in the bath, Raffaele pointing the water at the two normally grubby little boys. The water running down the plughole was dark and muddy from the three as they indulged in this new experience.

Wrapped in huge towels, the boys ran into Dolores' room, where she lay awake.

"We've had a shower!" Marco and Rico said in unison.

"I heard you." She sounded very sleepy. "You were making quite a noise."

"You should try it," said Raffaele. "It's much better than a bucket of cold water."

"I might just do that." She smiled at her three brothers, who were cleaner than they had ever been.

Within an hour, all the children had eaten breakfast and, under Raffaele's guidance, had packed their belongings and some food into various bags. Dolores had brought Isabella's medicine and gave her a dose before they left at seven-thirty.

It was with some sadness that they left the big house which had been their home for just one luxurious day. The area was so tidy and elegant, in sharp contrast to the run-down houses they had been used to all their lives, and when they returned to the shanty area, there was a noticeable hum of activity. Many children were carrying bags, presumably full of their belongings. Raffaele and his siblings followed the crowd, and very soon, the long school bus came into view.

Instead of the mournful queue waiting for the bus to take them to the drudgery that they called school, the children talked excitedly as they loaded the vehicle with as many bags as they could fit into every conceivable storage space. The bus was old and a bit battered in places, but to the children, it was magnificent—a magnet to everyone in the area.

"Raffaele!" Jose shouted. "I was hoping you would come. I've saved some seats for you near the front."

Within a few minutes, the family was sitting in the long, yellow school bus, eager for the adventure ahead of them. There were at least sixty noisy children squeezed into the bus, using every available seat. News of the planned journey to Florida had spread, and more children were turning up, hopeful of finding a space, but the bus was already over capacity by some twenty children.

"Come on, Pepe," Jose said. "We can't fit any more. Let's go."

"Okay, I think I'm ready. I hope you'll help with navigating, Jose."

"Yes, of course."

Pepe started the engine and, hoping he could remember everything his father had shown him, engaged the gears. The bus lurched forward, causing all the children to grab hold of any nearby rail for support. Pepe sounded the horn as more children appeared, running towards the bus in a desperate attempt to board the vehicle then standing in stunned silence as the bus drove on. Two brave eleven-year-old twin boys ran after it and jumped at the back, scrabbling to hold on. They climbed onto the top of the bus and clung to the edges of the vents. Worried about their safety, Pepe pulled over and helped the twins down from the roof. He didn't have the heart to leave them behind. Their delighted smiles showed that their gamble had paid off, and they happily squeezed themselves in at the back.

Pepe was sweating as he manoeuvred the heavy vehicle through the small roads and felt relieved when, at last, they reached Highway 85 heading north towards the border. Even then, he had to avoid the many vehicles which had crashed when their drivers disappeared. Pepe was exhilarated by the task of controlling such a powerful vehicle, finding it easier to keep in the fast lane of the four-lane highway. While driving, he showed Jose the various hand and foot controls in the hope that he could act as a reserve driver if necessary.

The children on the bus were excited at the prospect of actually being in Florida, and they chatted happily, imagining their new life away from the slums that had been their home since birth.

Raffaele asked Jose how long it would take to reach Orlando. The distance was about two thousand miles, and depending on how many obstacles they encountered, Jose estimated it would take at least a few days. After a while, the noise from the children abated as some gazed at the scenery while others fell asleep. In places, the four lanes reduced to only two, making it more difficult to pass the hundreds of wrecked cars dotted along the highway like some huge three-dimensional work of art.

After about four hours driving, Pepe pulled in at a rest stop, where those who needed to use the toilets did so. Pepe was exhausted from the strain of keeping in one position for a long time, and his arms ached from the effort of turning the large steering wheel. He knew his father would be proud of his effort, and the experience made him admire the man even more. It saddened him to think he would never see his parents again.

Pepe had been watching the fuel gauge, which indicated the tank was only one-third full. He was nervous about using the gas pump, as he had never done it before, but it was better to do it now than run dry in the middle of nowhere. Even locating the fuel cap took a while, but with the help of his friends, he managed to operate the pump. Best of all, there was nobody demanding money for the gallons of gas it took to fill the enormous tank of the aging bus.

After a break of about thirty minutes, Jose took his place at the steering wheel for the first time and started the engine, ready—with Pepe's guidance and supervision—for the next part of this strange journey.

After a jerky start, he soon gained in confidence and kept the big, yellow bus at a steady speed of fifty miles an hour through the baking afternoon sun. Jose drove skilfully and without tiredness; within a few hours, the journey became more mountainous, and the freeway widened to six lanes as they approached the Texas border.

It was a great relief when he spotted the border area at Nuevo Laredo in Texas. He had set the gauge at zero at the start of their journey and noted with pride that they had already driven over six hundred and fifty miles. But as they came closer to the border, he realised there was going to be a problem—not from security, now that the president and his border control no longer existed, but from the cars which had stopped at the crossing when the adults had disappeared.

Jose drew up, pulled on the handbrake and switched off the engine. There were about seven cars still waiting, and they would be waiting forever unless somebody did something about them.

Chapter Eleven:
End of a Long Journey

PEPE, JOSE AND Raffaele looked glumly at the obstacles in front of them. The border control point was bad enough, but the cars blocking their way seemed impenetrable.

"What are we going to do?" asked Raffaele.

Pepe was a resourceful youth and was determined not to be beaten by any physical obstacle. "We move them!"

This declaration took his friends by surprise.

"How?" asked Jose.

"Children power. With enough of us pushing, we could do it. Get all the stronger boys together and we can do it."

Very soon, fifteen of the bigger boys were gathered in the road. After releasing the handbrakes, they managed with their combined strength to push the cars out of the way. Everybody cheered as the boys, sweating from their exertions, climbed back on board the bus.

There was an even bigger cheer when Pepe, taking over from Jose, started the engine and slowly took the bus forward, officially crossing the border between Mexico and the State of Texas in the United States of America. Best of all, nobody attempted to stop them. In the past, the president's border guards would have strictly patrolled the area ensuring that hopeful immigrants from Mexico were turned back: over the past two years, many of those attempting to breach the border would have been shot dead.

All the children looked with interest at the scenery as they drove northwards through an area which none of them had ever expected to visit. It was now becoming quite dark, and the teenagers agreed that they should stop for the night and get some rest. Pepe turned off the highway and looked for somewhere to park. A wooded area provided shelter where they could stay overnight. It was a case of trying to relax in the confined space of the bus, the seats seeming more uncomfortable with the passing of time.

Drinks and snacks were shared between the children, but not surprisingly, it proved difficult for most of the children to sleep soundly. Dolores gave Isabella more medicine and was relieved that the infant seemed to be improving, even taking an interest in this strangest of journeys. Dolores was as excited as all the other children and thought back to her miserable life before the adults had disappeared. She was pleased her father was gone forever but wished her mother was with them; she would have felt much better and safer.

The next morning, as soon as the sun appeared, Pepe was behind the wheel, ready to start the second day's long journey. The teenager drove the bus back onto the freeway, heading north for San Antonio along Interstate 35.

They had not been driving for long when one of the children spotted something through the window. "What's that?"

Unlike everything else, this was something moving and, worryingly, heading in their direction. It seemed to be taller than all the surrounding buildings and was moving quite fast.

It was Raffaele who realised with horror what it was. "That's a tornado!"

Heads turned to watch the fast-approaching column of swirling air. Texas was notorious for tornados, which regularly created havoc, and this was no exception. Debris was being lifted high and cars were pushed aside like toys as the danger drew ever closer. Many of the children made the sign of the cross, praying for divine intervention.

Pepe put his foot down hard on the accelerator, hoping beyond hope that they could escape the danger. The children screamed as the giant twister came ever closer and then rammed the rear of the bus. The jolt was tremendous, and for a moment, Pepe feared they would be tipped over, but as the tornado crossed their path, they were still upright, still moving forward, shaken but unhurt. Everybody watched with relief as the angry twister continued on its destructive path eastwards.

Hoping this would be the only tornado they encountered, they continued along the Pan-Am Expressway for another two hours before they reached the city of San Antonio. Some of the children recognised the significance of the city from their history lessons at school. It was here, at the Alamo, where their ancestors had initially defeated the Texans in 1836, only to be defeated themselves a couple of months later.

In contrast to the dry, dusty Texan landscape through which they had been travelling, San Antonio was a large, pleasant, metropolitan area with a wide river running through the centre of the city. Pepe was relieved when he spotted the intersection and turned, heading eastwards towards New Orleans.

Many children who had been looting stores stared in amazement as the packed school bus passed them by. The fact that it was the only moving vehicle they had seen for the last few days was enough for several tough-looking teenagers to run towards it.

Pepe kept his foot hard down, fearing these strangers would rob them of their only transport. Thankfully, the teenagers were unable to catch up with the bus.

It was a relief when the sprawling city gave way to the vast expanse of countryside.

By this time, many of the younger children were becoming restless, as they had not expected the journey to take so long, believing they would be in Orlando in just a few hours. Pepe had kept a steady speed along the freeway, but the old bus was unable to travel at more than sixty miles an hour. Even then, the engine was straining, and after another couple of hours, it started to make rhythmic, clanking noises.

"What's that?" asked Jose.

"I don't know, but it's getting louder," answered Pepe. "I wonder if the tornado did some damage to the transmission."

"The question is, will it get us to Orlando? We're only halfway there."

Mile after mile, the old school bus struggled on, the noises from the engine getting ever louder.

Then Jose spotted a possible solution. "Look! Pull in over there, Pepe!"

Realising what Jose had in mind, the teenager braked hard and swung the bus off the freeway into a service area. He drew up close to three parked Greyhound buses and switched off the engine. "We had better check them before we transfer."

Easing out of the cramped driver's seat, he shouted so that everybody in the bus could hear him. "I want you all to stay here until we've checked to see if we can move to a better bus, as this one is struggling to keep going. Okay?"

Leaving Raffaele in charge, the older teenagers climbed down the steps and looked at the three smart Greyhound buses. Together, they went to the first of the three and tried the door. To their dismay, it stayed firmly shut.

"I hope they're not all locked," said Jose glumly.

It was a great relief when the door of the second bus opened with ease. They quickly climbed aboard.

"Great!" Pepe exclaimed. "The key's in the ignition." He jumped into the driver's seat and turned the key. The engine coughed to life. "The controls are more complicated than on the school bus, but I'm sure between us, we can master them."

"Check the fuel level," Jose advised.

Pepe scanned the various indicators and spotted the fuel gauge. "It's about half full, I think."

"Let's check the last bus. It might have more."

"Good idea!" Pepe turned off the engine, and the boys ran to the third bus. Again, the door was unlocked and the key in the ignition. When the engine started, the gauge indicated three-quarters full. "I guess this is the one we should take."

Jose looked concerned. The bus was more modern than the other two. "Are you sure you can drive this bus, Pepe?"

"No!" A wide smile lit Pepe's face. "But I can try. Just don't expect me to reverse this thing!"

Jose laughed. "I'll transfer the children while you get used to the controls."

The younger boy returned to the school bus and collected most of the children, together with all their possessions and what food was left. Meanwhile, Raffaele led a smaller group to the store, where they stocked up with drinks, biscuits, chocolate bars and anything else they could find. He felt a twinge of conscience as he plundered the store but quickly dismissed it. No adults would ever be back to discover their crime.

As they climbed into the Greyhound bus with their new provisions, many commented on the luxury of this modern transport compared to the old school bus. The seats were softer and more comfortable, so much more suitable for long journeys. A bonus was the on-board toilet, which for some reason was very popular with the excited and curious youngsters.

Pepe took a deep breath and loosened the handbrake while moving into drive mode. Steering back onto the freeway, he set off for New Orleans. Many of the children waved fondly at the old yellow without which they could not have escaped Mexico and entered North America.

The Greyhound bus was much faster, making the long journey pass much quicker as they sped along the road for mile after mile.

Remembering how teenagers had posed a threat to them at San Antonio, Pepe maintained his speed as he drove through New Orleans, keeping an eye on intersections where they had to turn.

"Can you look out for the junction for Interstate 10 to Mobile, Alabama, Jose?"

"Okay, no problem." Jose looked with interest at the area they were passing through. Although he was too young to remember much about it, he knew about Hurricane Katrina and its devastating effects on the city. Many lives had been lost, and the damage to property had taken many years to recover from. He'd also learned at school that New Orleans was famous for its jazz music; without adults to perform it, the legacy could disappear for good—unless the city's young people continued the tradition. They did see quite a few children, all understandably surprised by the sight of a solitary Greyhound racing through their streets.

Both Pepe and Jose spotted the intersection at the same time, and they headed eastwards towards Mobile. Jose took over driving from Pepe, stopping in the middle of a sparsely populated area to avoid any possible confrontation by jealous children. From Mobile, they continued towards Pensacola, which to their relief, was in the state of Florida. They still had some 450 miles to go and decided to stop again for the night. Many of the younger children had become disenchanted with the lengthy journey. It took a while to settle down for the night, but eventually, the packed bus fell silent allowing Pepe and Jose to get a well-earned rest.

As soon as the sun rose the next morning, Pepe stood up, stretched his legs and took the wheel again, ready for what would, hopefully, be the last leg of their journey.

After a while travelling east, they passed through Florida's state capital, Tallahassee, and a while later joined Interstate 75. From there, it was a further two hours' south to Orlando.

Excitement aboard the bus mounted when they spotted the first signs for Disneyworld and Universal Studios, excited for their stay in this renowned magical corner of the world. Pepe noticed the gauge indicated only a little gas left in the tank, but he kept it to himself, hoping it would be enough to reach their destination.

When they drove onto Universal Boulevard, they knew they were almost at the end of their journey, and the children cheered loudly as they drove through the entrance to Universal Studios theme park.

Pepe pulled up near the ticket barriers, switched off the engine and leaned back in his seat, breathing a huge sigh of relief. "We did it!"

Jose stood up at the front of the bus, like some official tourist guide. "Okay, everybody. From here, you're on your own. If there's any food left on the bus, take it with you, as we have no idea how much food there will be here."

The children rose from their seats, uncertain at first, and moved along the bus towards the exit. One of the twins handed a couple of biscuits to Jose and Pepe, saying, "Give a tip to the drivers, everybody!"

Although this was said jokingly, the children gave another loud cheer for the two teenagers who, together, had driven them nearly two thousand miles from Mexico to Orlando.

All climbed down from the bus, carrying what few possessions they had, and headed for the gates. Somebody had already broken most of the turnstiles, allowing easy entry with no need for a ticket.

The Mexican children all had big smiles as they swarmed through the turnstiles, happy to be in the place they had dreamed of until this day. Even the fact that not all attractions were working did not dampen their spirits.

The younger children walked through to Disneyworld, while the older ones were happy to stay within Universal. Some seventeen-year-olds had taken responsibility for keeping the attractions running by making certain the tracks were kept clear to avoid collisions. Even so, there were accidents, and without adult medical care, the children's injuries went unattended until some of the older children managed to find first-aid kits.

Raffaele, as head of his family, stayed close to his brothers and sisters to protect them and stop them from becoming lost and afraid. Pepe and Jose, realising the possible danger in having masses of uncontrollable children wandering around, joined the ranks of the other teenagers effectively acting as park wardens.

The other problem was the shortage of food, which was already causing fights for valuable food supplies, and it could only get worse.

Chapter Twelve:
Arrival

Alex, Charles, Cassy and the two children were making good headway, their main obstacles being the mass of vehicles that had crashed after their drivers had disappeared. Alex had become quite expert at manoeuvring the car around these roadblocks; even so, when Universal Boulevard came into view, they were all relieved to be nearing the end of their strange and eventful journey.

A few minutes later, the entrance gates to the theme park came into view, and Alex took the car in at a leisurely pace. As expected, there were no adults to stop them, and Alex kept going until he reached one of the big hotels and pulled up close to the building.

"Why here?" asked Cassy.

"We need a base, and these hotels must have plenty of empty rooms. If we stay on the first level, we can keep our food secure yet still get out in a hurry if the lifts stop working."

"Good idea!" Charles said, thinking of the luxury suites now available to them all.

Alex and Charles picked up a box of food each and ensured that the remainder was securely locked in the boot. The last thing they wanted was to lose their precious provisions to greedy survivors.

The entrance hall at the Hard Rock Hotel was very spacious and weirdly quiet with nobody to greet them. The only clues to anyone ever having been there were the suitcases and piles of shoes and clothes dotted around the large area.

Charles walked up to the reception desk, thumped his hand on the hard surface and said in a demanding tone, "Come on, we need some service around here!"

Alex and Cassy laughed, amused by Charles's antics.

"You'll have a long wait before you can get checked in," Cassy said.

A broad smile lit Charles's face. "I'm pretty certain the rooms will only open with authorised plastic cards, so if we're to have any chance of getting in, we'll need a master key. Help me look, please."

Cassy and Alex were suitably impressed by Charles's logical mind. The three of them began to search the drawers in the huge desk.

It was Alex who found the place where the master key cards were kept. He took out six and distributed them to the others.

Ignoring the lifts, the group climbed the stairs to the first floor.

"I suggest we find three rooms next to each other," Alex said, looking along the wide corridor. "It's better if we stick together."

They agreed and began trying the key cards on each door. None of the rooms they opened had any occupants, so they took their time until they located three of the superior rooms.

191

They were quite noisy as they called out to each other, and to add to the noise, Angela was crying loudly. Cassy was hoping to get settled quickly so she could feed the infant.

At the same time, Jason, Rebecca and the two children had returned to the hotel after collecting some food from the restaurants. They were surprised to hear the new voices as they entered the lobby.

"They sound English," Rebecca said. "Let's go and meet them."

Jason was a little reluctant but agreed with his sister.

The voices became clearer as they drew closer.

Alex was just coming out of one room when he spotted the other group. "Hi! These aren't your rooms, are they?"

Jason answered. "No. Ours are on the seventh floor. We heard you from the lobby and wondered who was here."

Alex called Cassy and Charles to come and meet the other children.

"Where were you when all the adults disappeared?" Rebecca asked.

"We were on our flight," Cassy answered. "Just approaching Orlando airport. There were only a few of us who survived, as we had to jump before the plane crashed."

"You jumped?" Jason's surprise was very evident. "How *did* you survive?"

Charles laughed. "We were extremely lucky. I still find it hard to believe we only got a few scratches." After a moment's thought, he added, "We have Alex to thank for that. He was the only person who actually did anything to keep us alive, unlike all those poor devils who were too frightened to jump."

Alex blushed at Charles's words of praise. "I couldn't have done it without Cassy. She's been a fantastic help. How about you guys? Where were you when the adults disappeared?"

"Nothing as exciting as your experience," Jason said. "We'd already been here a few days and were actually in our hotel room at the time."

Seeing her brother wince with guilt, Rebecca took over. "Since then, we've been helping some of the many children we came across as well as finding what food we can. I don't know what will happen to us when all the food runs out."

Charles, always the one to lighten the atmosphere, said, "Don't worry. Between us, we'll look for a good supply. There's plenty of land around here where we can plant potatoes and other vegetables. I don't suppose Walt Disney would approve, but who cares?"

The ginger-haired teenager made the others laugh, and for the time being, their situation didn't seem quite so bad.

Chapter Thirteen:
Meeting Point

THE TWO GROUPS had agreed to meet up the following day to see what was still working in the theme parks. They carried snacks and drinks, which they shared equally. The temperature was in the high eighties, and the sun shone down relentlessly on the British children. Remarkably, many of the air-conditioned, indoor attractions were still functioning, giving them relief from the intense summer heat.

Alex had been hoping to go on the Duelling Dragons, but much to his disappointment, as a high maintenance ride, it stood eerily silent and unmoving.

Hogwarts was, however, still functioning with the voices of the characters from Harry Potter welcoming the children. The normally neat, orderly lines were non-existent, since there were no adults to keep them under control.

Shops in Diagon Alley were fascinating, most of the children pocketing some of the better-tasting sweets. Jason was especially intrigued by Ollivander's Wand shop and the vast array of wands; he wished he could use one to bring back the adults.

Everybody laughed when Charles appeared in a Death Eater mask, apart from Danny, who was very frightened.

Charles quickly took off the mask to ease the little boy's fear.

The children were excited to see Platform 9 ¾ for the train to Hogwarts but disappointed to find that the train was immobile and silent. Alex, who had visited a few years earlier and remembered the cacophony of noise in the huge station, longed to recreate the former level of excitement for the Hogwarts Express in this magical world.

The group was luckier in the Skull Island Reign of Kong area, where they were able to sit in the transport vehicle, supposedly travelling over the prehistoric plains, with images of rare creatures roaming the land, all cleverly achieved by the use of huge television screens taking the place of the vehicle's windows.

It was late in the afternoon when the children made their way back towards their hotel, yet the heat was still baking the ground.

As they neared the hotel, they were surprised to hear what sounded like a fairly large vehicle. Uncertain what it may be and what danger it may present, the children hid behind an outbuilding to observe without being seen.

They were amazed when a Greyhound bus drove through the entrance gates into the large, open area and came to a stop. After a couple of minutes, children started to emerge from the bus, looking tired yet happy and excited.

After a hastily whispered discussion, Alex, Cassy, Charles, Jason and Rebecca decided the newcomers did not present a threat and agreed to meet the new group. They approached the bus and were amazed to see how many children had been crammed inside.

Alex spoke first, saying "Hello! Where are you all from?"

Nobody answered. Some of the children stopped and stared at him, but from the chatter of others, which sounded like Spanish, he guessed they were from a South American country.

Three older boys climbed down from the bus and walked up to the British group.

"Hello!" Charles greeted them. "Who drove the Greyhound bus?"

Pepe answered in English. "I did, together with my friend, Jose." He indicated one of the boys next to him, then the other. "This is Raffaele, and I'm Pepe."

The British children were impressed.

"Where have you driven from?" asked Charles.

"Mexico City. It has taken three days for us to travel two thousand miles."

"That's amazing!" said Alex. "I don't think I could have driven such a great distance."

With most of the Mexican children able to speak some English, soon the children were all chatting and sharing stories.

Charles, as always, saw the humour in the situation. "The president would be hopping mad if he could hear us now. Thankfully, he's no longer around to stop people doing what they should always have been able to."

The conversation turned to the theme parks, and the British children explained that many of the attractions were no longer working. This did not seem to dampen the enthusiasm of the newcomers, who went off to investigate for themselves.

Chapter Fourteen:
A Deadly Conclusion

MUCH AS JASON liked the USA—the Hard Rock Hotel and Universal Studios in particular—he could not envisage spending the rest of his life in this artificial world designed mainly for children.

It had been a relief to meet Alex, Cassy, Charles and, by now, around sixty Mexican children, yet it was not enough to lift his sorrowful mood.

Wondering what his future held, he walked slowly with Rebecca and Peter towards their hotel room. It did, at least, give him some sense of security to return to the same place where this strangeness had started three days earlier.

Jason flopped onto his bed, his depression deepening. He still blamed himself for the demise of the adult population.

Rebecca, by contrast, was optimistic and believed that somehow, the world would survive and hopefully in the not-too-distant future return to one of reasonable normality.

Noticing how messy their room was, she began clearing the piles of food cartons and bottles, taking them to one of the empty rooms.

As she was tidying her parents' room, her eyes fell on a newspaper lying on a cabinet at the side of the bed.

It was the one her dad had been reading when he disappeared, and it was folded to highlight a particular article. Curious, Rebecca picked it up and began to read.

More than 10,000 scientists from all over the world, after many years of development and testing, are about to switch on the new 'FCC'—Future Circular Collider—in CERN, Switzerland. The 100 km circular collider will create billions of Higgs Bosons and trillions of quarks, creating new opportunities to study rare decays and flavour physics benefitting from higher collision energies.

Operating at -271°C, the FCC will help scientists understand dark matter, which accounts for around 25% of the visible universe, and the prevalence of matter over anti-matter.

However, a British physicist, Professor Jeremy Bollinger, together with other eminent scientists, has serious doubts about the safety of such experiments and has been trying, in vain, to prevent the switch-on of the FCC.

Through his studies, Bollinger claims to have discovered that the probable effect of the most-powerful collisions of sub-atomic particles would be either to completely destroy matter or transfer it through wormholes to outer parts of the universe or even other dimensions.

Of one thing Professor Bollinger is quite certain: "The FCC's effect will be catastrophic. While younger, still-developing humans *may* survive, all mature human tissue will disappear instantly without trace, leaving juveniles in charge of the world."

Rebecca called Jason over to look at the newspaper article. Both were stunned to discover that the switch-on of the FCC had been scheduled for Monday, 31st July 2023: the day that all adults had suddenly and tragically disappeared.

About the Author

John Stephen Raynor, born in 1944 in Oldham, Lancashire, was diagnosed with a serious progressive eye condition, retinitis pigmentosa.

At fifteen, he began working in architecture, eventually becoming a self-employed software developer and marrying his first wife in 1967. Sadly, the long hours building up his business took their toll, and the couple separated in 1989.

It was in the Philippines he found his soul mate, whom he married in 1993. Her experiences are the inspiration for much of John's fictional work, including his first novel, *A Comfortable Death*.

After twenty years of keeping diaries, John drew on these to publish *A Chronicle of Intimacies*, followed by *Who wants to be British?* – the two autobiographical works describing his most traumatic period.

Registered blind since the age of thirty-five, John relies on his computer with speech synthesis for software development and creative writing.

Also by J. S. Raynor

Novels

A Comfortable Death

In the land of Ferdinand Marcos, you quickly learn to be tough. Lisa was the eighth child in the poverty-stricken Tiguelo family. Born in the Philippine province of Cotobata during 1965, she was to learn just how difficult life could be. This touching yet thrilling story describes the turbulent life of stunningly beautiful Lisa through her troublesome  childhood to joining the New People's Army at fifteen and, later, her mission to avenge her grandmother's death.

The Gaudi Façade

Adam Sheldrake, a young British architect, travels to Barcelona for what should be a fairly ordinary holiday. By chance, he meets beautiful, talented, twenty-seven-year-old Italian artist Caterina Fonteras at the Olympic Stadium, and from this point, the holiday turns into a life-changing experience for both of them.

With a common interest in Antoni Gaudi, the famous Spanish architect, they visit the Sagrada Família and are drawn into a world of violent fanaticism, resulting in their capture and imprisonment. This romantic thriller, set in the year 2012, leads the reader into many twists and turns, a major threat to the Catholic faith and some quite extraordinary revelations.

See All Evil

When British soldier, Alex McCloud is injured and blinded in Afghanistan during 2011, he is offered the chance of sight using bionic implants, developed by Professor Goldman of Moorfields Eye Hospital in London, in conjunction with Augmented Reality specialist, Major Jennifer Sherlock of the CIA.

These implants not only provide him with sight but much, much more, proving to be of great interest both to the MOD and the CIA. His new life as an intelligence officer based in London brings him many challenges utilising his unique abilities.

Autobiographical Works

A Chronicle of Intimacies

It was 1991 and John Raynor's life was in a mess. At forty-six, two years after separating from his wife, he was living on his own and the future seemed very bleak.

And then, there was Carol, a divorcee two years younger than him. Suddenly, everything changed, hopefully for the better. The bond was immediate and intense. The problem was that one day, Carol would need John, both physically and emotionally, while the next, she would be secretive, cool and distant.

This is the true account of a sixteen-month relationship which turned John's life upside down, with the added complexity of him being registered blind. During this period, he travelled to Paris, Amsterdam and Singapore and made close friends with Wendy, Angeline, Jasmine, Mirz, Amanda and Sarah, but Carol had stolen his heart. Everything is factual, except for Carol's true identity.

Who wants to be British?

Following on from the turbulent events described in *A Chronicle of Intimacies*, John Raynor's luck seemed, at last, to be turning in his favour. In January, 1993, he flew from Manchester to the Philippines to meet Aleth Ledres, a Filipina twenty-three years younger than him. The two had been writing for several months,

and within a short space of time, they fell in love and their marriage was planned for April. Unfortunately, nothing was ever simple for John and Aleth, as many problems seem to prevent them from enjoying a life together in the UK. Cultural differences, the Catholic Church and British immigration officials all seemed destined to destroy any chance of future happiness. This true account of the couple's romantic adventures echoes the uncanny forecasts of the psychic's predictions.

Find out more about John's previous and upcoming works on his website: www.jsraynor.co.uk

Beaten Track Publishing

For more titles from Beaten Track Publishing,
please visit our website:

https://www.beatentrackpublishing.com

Thanks for reading!